STRIKE HIM OUT

Strike Him Out!

By Harold M. Sherman

The Goldsmith Publishing Co.

CHICAGO

Publisher's Preface

◉ ◉ ◉

WE ARE again fortunate in being able to present to American youth another fine story by Harold M. Sherman.

This popular author of boys books needs no introduction to the vast majority of young readers. His splendid tales of sport and school life abound in all the things that appeal most to every red-blooded boy. Every one of them sparkles with the clean fun and excitement that are an integral part of American school life. The gridiron, the baseball diamond, the track;—Harold M. Sherman knows them all. Above all he knows boys; what they like and do not like. His heroes are the finest examples of sturdy American youth, lovers of sport and sportsmanship without being, in any sense of the word, "sissies."

To those of our young readers who have read that stirring tale of college and football field, "Over The Line," we need say no more. To those of you who are meeting our author for the first time in "Strike Him Out," will come the genuine pleasure of meeting real boys and real sport.

To boys who like, as every red-blooded boy must, this kind of thing, we dedicate this book, that they may receive entertainment and inspiration from this story.

THE GOLDSMITH PUBLISHING CO.

CONTENTS

CHAPTER I

THE GOAT GETTER

"BETTER look out, Speed. Bimbo's laying for you!"

The warning came from Salty Peters, veteran centerfielder of North High's baseball nine and was addressed to Bob "Speed" Durgan, fellow team-mate, who was regarded as the greatest pitcher in the history of the school.

"Laying for me, eh?" repeated Speed. "Where'd you hear that?"

"It's being noised all over town," was Salty's reply. "The old reign of terror's starting again just because it's near the start of baseball season. South Side can't beat us unless they get our goats and that's what they're out to do!"

Speed nodded, grimly.

"They've gotten the breaks the last couple of years, that's a fact."

"Breaks? Say, they just naturally scared us out of the games!" ranted Salty. "Last year that human bull, Bimbo, got you so upset you uncorked a wild pitch that sent in their winning run! And maybe that South Side crowd wasn't tickled! They're the only outfit that's been able to beat your pitching!"

"They won't do it this season!" vowed Speed, grimly.

"Well, you'll have to get the ball past that fence busting Bimbo Bailey, then!" countered Salty. "And you'll have to watch your step before the game because he and his gang will try to put the fear of devils in us—especially in you—since you're the guy they've got to stack up against in the pitcher's box!"

"I'm wise to that Bimbo," said Speed, as he kicked a stone from the campus of North High. "He's a tough bozo all right. About time our fellows were making a real stand against his gang. Just because they run the south side of town is no reason why they should be running the north!"

Salty shrugged his shoulders, helplessly. "Well, Napoleon wasn't satisfied to stay in his own country—and Bimbo isn't, either. It tickles him pink to get us on the run. I'd hate to meet that baby in a lonely spot at night, myself. What shoulders and what a chest he's got! And those arms of his—he could just about break a guy in two. Remember the time he caught Teaser Burke and gave him a knuckle rub? Teaser couldn't bear a hat on his head for three weeks after that!"

"What you trying to do—give me something to worry about?" accused Speed, forcing a grin. "I know Bimbo as well as you do—and better! He's been after me before."

"Yeah, but maybe he hasn't meant business like he does now," went on Salty. "I understand he's worked out some kind of a secret order with his bunch and that they're just itching to initiate the leader of the North Side crowd, which happens to be *you!*"

Speed stared into space for a moment. "I can begin to see now," he said, with conviction, "why you fellows picked me as captain. You had a sneaking hunch that whoever might be holding down that position would be Bimbo's target. Well, that being the case, I resign right now!"

Salty laughed. "You can't do that," he declared. "You're in for it! But have no fear— we'll stand behind you!"

"How far behind?" asked Speed, incredulously.

"Well . . ." hesitated Salty, "that . . . er . . . depends on how close Bimbo is to you! The closer he is, the further behind we'll be!"

"I thought so," rejoined Speed, wryly. "That's very encouraging, Salty. Very! I feel just as safe now as though I was standing on a bomb with the fuse lit."

"You *are* just as safe!" assured Salty, grinning.

"Hey!" cried Speed. "Cut it! This is getting to be a sore subject with me."

"Okay—but just the same—I wouldn't venture over on the other side of town any more than I had to, if I were you!"

Speed's face colored.

"You mean my calling on Marjory Coulter?"

"How'd you guess it?" joshed Salty. "Marjory's a nice girl but since she's moved to South Oakland, Bimbo's taken a shine to her . . . and if that doesn't mean trouble for you, then sticky fly paper never hurt a fly."

"But she wouldn't have anything to do with him!" said Speed, confidently.

"She wouldn't, eh?" retorted Salty, with less faith in woman kind. "Don't forget, she's going to South High now instead of North. And she was out rooting for Bimbo during football season and rooting for South to beat us!"

"That's only natural," defended Speed. "She has to be loyal to the school she's attending. But she's one of my best friends. She ought to be, our families living next door to each other so many years. Marj may root for South but she's just as glad if we win . . . and she's always pulling for me to . . . er . . . put up a good game."

"I see," said Salty, eyes twinkling. "Well, I'm glad to get the low-down on that. I was afraid Marj might be using you to get information on us and pass on to the enemy. Women are pretty smart that way, you know. Got to watch out for 'em!"

"Say—if there was anything to tell it would be just the other way around!" declared Speed, spiritedly. "I'm going to be taking her to the Costume Ball tonight and I'll ask her if she knows anything about what Bimbo's up to. Maybe it would be a good thing if she paid a little attention to him. She might be able to tip us off. That's a good suggestion you made, Salty—that spy business!"

Salty looked pleased and quite puffed up.

"Oh, I have an idea or two once in awhile," he answered. "That's why the boys picked me to sound you out—see how you felt about Bimbo—and what you were going to do about it!"

"Oh, is that so?" rejoined Speed, a bit taken aback. "So the fellows feel that it's up to me to save their hides, do they? Isn't that nice? . . . Well, if we can't get organized to stand together any better than we have in the past, it's going to be every man for himself. I'm not going to absorb the punishment for the gang—so kindly disabuse the boys of that idea right here and now!"

Speed was earnest in this declaration as humorous as it may have sounded. Just because he was leader of the North Side crowd, he did not care to have Bimbo center an attack upon him. The king of the South Side had caused him enough trouble already. There wasn't a fellow in all of Oakland who did not have a whole-

some respect for his physical prowess and Bimbo
knew it. On the baseball diamond, Carl
"Bimbo" Bailey was a real star—a fine out-
fielder and murderous batsman. Scarcely a
game went by that he did not hit the ball out of
the park and he was the only batter who actually
had the "Indian sign" on pitcher Speed Durgan. North High might have an excellent ball
team with an enviable record of victories, as had
been the case the past two seasons, but a meeting
with South High meant disappointment and
defeat.

"Our boys just seem to go to pieces against
the South bunch," a North Side rooter remarked. "They're feared by every other team
they meet and Speed Durgan turns in finely
pitched games . . . but let Bimbo Bailey lead
his South Side gang from the dugout to do battle
and we're licked at the start. Must be an inferiority complex or something because we beat
better teams during the season than South has.
Here's hoping our boys snap out of it this year
and turn the tables. It's Speed's last year in
North High and he deserves a victory over this
scrappy outfit!"

For years a state of feud had existed between the north and south sides of Oakland, this rivalry expressing itself particularly in the sports attitude of the two high schools. Oakland originally existed on but one side of the Kent river and its growth to almost equal size on the north side made separate schools as well as separate business districts necessary. The old part of town then commenced taking issue with the new part of town and the friendly competition had continued through the years. To the younger element a crossing of the bridge over the Kent river was to invite danger. Not that something was certain to befall youths from either side of town who found themselves on the other side but something very easily *could* happen were the gangs on one side mischief bent, desirous of avenging some real or fancied slight.

"We North Siders have got to watch our step," was a decision early arrived at by citizens of the new part of town. "We're not so well organized or physically strong as South—and the only chance we've got to come out on top is by matching our wits against their brawn!"

Bimbo Bailey, present leader of the South Side gang, knew very well that he held the advantageous position. Perhaps never before had South possessed such power. He ruled his fellows with an iron hand, taking this phrase from history and applying it to himself.

"Every great leader down through the ages used iron hand methods," Bimbo told his lieutenants at one inspired meeting. "That's the only way to make your followers respect you and obey your orders—by laying down the law and laying it down heavy. So if I seem hardboiled, just remember—I'm doing it to get results! As for the North Side gang—all we got to do to run them is to keep 'em scared of us. Every so often it's up to us to pull something that will leave them gasping. Take their leader, Speed Durgan. I've got him so he'll jump through hoops backwards. But you can't let him go too long . . . you got to give him another dose . . . and he's about due now! He's coming over on this side of town too much—calling on this Marjory Coulter. That's got to stop!"

The word 'got' was very necessary to Bimbo's vocabulary. It was the shortest way he knew to convey something which had to be done. And his comrades were able to understand the three letter word perfectly.

"Just as you say, Chief!" responded Lieutenant Sam Wade. "What'll we do—catch him and cut off his ears?"

"No, that's too barbarian!" grinned Bimbo. "Let's begin with his toes!"

"You mean—cut 'em off?"

"No—step on 'em!" said Bimbo, still grinning.

There were snickers from his gang members. Their reign of terror had consisted mostly of threats of violence which had never materialized. Last time they had captured Speed Durgan he had been made to walk a plank, blind-folded, which he believed extended out over the Kent River. Commanded to jump he had crouched on the plank and begged for mercy only to be prodded by a merciless Bimbo.

"Afraid of a ducking, eh? It's lucky for you we didn't tie you hand and foot! You've swam this river before. Let's see you do it again and when you get on the other side—stay there— where you belong!"

Speed had finally mustered up courage enough to jump, landing not in the river, as he had expected, but in a huge mud puddle. And, on being released, he had slunk away greatly humiliated that he had betrayed any fear whatsoever at anything the enemy might have threatened to do to him.

"I want Speed Durgan to see our new Torture Chamber," declared Bimbo. "He should be flattered to know we've built it specially for him."

"I'll say!" exclaimed Sam. "He'll probably appreciate it—*not!* Great idea of yours—us fixing up a place under that new building. If we're careful nobody can figure out where we are!"

"That's the point," emphasized Bimbo. "With the back end of this building built up on steel framework, it gives us a chance for the swellest sort of a hangout underneath . . . like we're in some big cavern of girders."

"You get kind of a weird feeling under the building at night," said Stub Hanley. "I do, anyhow! . . . Gee! Sometimes I get to wondering—what if that building would collapse?

It's up there in the air, six stories off the ground in back, before the building begins at all! Now if there'd be an earthquake. . . . !"

"Aw, you're always worrying about something that never happens! This isn't earthquake country!" rejoined Bimbo. "Besides, that building's as safe as any other. Just because it's built on a slope so's the back end has to be raised even with the front of the building which is on the top of the hill, doesn't mean anything. I know it looks like you might push the whole thing over but those girders are all sunk in solid rock and reinforced with concrete!"

"Okay! If you're willing to risk having the building fall on you, so am I!" acceded Stub.

"Getting back to Speed Durgan!" said Bimbo, dryly. "North Side is holding a big St. Patrick's Night Costume Ball this evening. And something tells me that Speed is going to be there . . . unless we change his mind for him."

"What do you mean—'something tells you'?" asked Sam.

Bimbo flashed a wise smile. "I heard so from good authority," he answered. "Thought I'd take Marjory to a picture show tonight but she said she had a previous engagement!"

"Oh, ho!" laughed the gang.

"And what did you say to that?" joshed Kinky Roxburg.

"I told her I hoped nothing came up to break that engagement but, if something unexpected *did* happen, would she then like to go to the picture show?"

"Yes? . . . Yes?" cried the bunch, eagerly.

"She said she was sure nothing would come up to change her plans and 'thanks very much' but she would have to go to the show with me some other time if I wanted her."

"Well, that's only fair," temporized Kinky. "A date is a date. Besides, that Costume Ball is one of the biggest events of the year on the North Side. I see by the paper that they're giving a hundred dollar prize for the best get-up."

"Some class! Wish we could try for it!"

"We can't, so that's that!" snapped Bimbo, eyes gleaming. "But there's one thing we can do if we can get hold of Speed . . ."

"What's that?"

"We can fix it so he won't have a chance at the prize!"

"Great!"

"Yeah, if we could only catch him in costume!"

"Thing to do is waylay him before he gets to Marjory's home," plotted Bimbo. "He'll probably be dressed for the party."

"Yes, and he'll probably be driving his Dad's car," surmised Sam. "What we going to do about that?"

Bimbo debated a moment. "We'll have to hide behind the hedge in Marjory's yard," he decided, finally. "And grab Speed as he parks his car and comes in the gate. There's enough of us so we can scoot him around the side of the house, out of sight, and into the alley before he can say, 'Jack Robinson.' Fact is, we mustn't let him make so much as a sound. I'll have my folks' car in the alley and we'll rush our victim to the Torture Chamber where we'll give him the third degree and fix his costume for him!"

"Isn't this going to be pretty stiff treatment?" asked Kinky, dubiously.

"Oh, we'll be through with him in half an hour and then he can go to the Costume Ball if he wants to," said Bimbo, smugly. "But, after this, I have an idea he'll be taking a girl who lives on his side of town!"

Billboards and newspapers in Oakland were heralding the arrival of Spring. It was the seventeenth of March, two days after Spring was officially supposed to have arrived, and the warm weather brought the feel of baseball in the air. At least this feeling was communicated to the athletes at North and South High schools who unearthed balls and gloves and engaged in preliminary practice. But the older generation saw in Spring's arrival only the opportunity and necessity for a "Paint Up and Clean Up!" campaign. It was this activity of Spring which the billboards and newspapers were stressing— an activity, too, which hardware dealers, paint stores, roofing establishments and fence concerns were making much ado over. And fond parents, impressed by certain home needs, were taking advantage of their sons' natural desire for sport exercise by substituting rakes and paint brushes in place of bats and balls—not always, it must be confessed, with the enthusiastic approval of the younger element.

"Bob," admonished Mr. Durgan, head of

the Durgan Paint Shop, on coming home from the store and finding his son preparing for the Costume Ball. "I see you're doing a lot of dressing up so I have a good job for you. To-morrow I'm sending some cans of paint to the house and you can get busy dressing it up in a new coat. How's that appeal to you?"

Speed tried to conceal his dejection.

"Why, er . . . a . . . that's great! The old house needs a new coat, doesn't it?"

"I can't say that it actually does," smiled Mr. Durgan. "But, being in the paint business, I've got to paint my home more often to impress the neighbors. Sort of set a good example. The more folks I can get to paint up . . ."

"Yeah, I know," broke in Speed. "The more money you'll make! I remember that from last year. It took me three weeks, working all my spare time . . . and here it's almost baseball season . . . !"

"Perhaps, then, you can work out a system to *throw* the paint on!" suggested his parent.

Speed grinned.

"I'd rather work out a system to *throw* the job," he rejoined. "But if you're satisfied with the way the house looks when I get through painting it—okay. Myself, I can't see that it's much of an advertisement!"

With this, Speed went on with the getting into his costume. He had rented the garb supposedly worn by an Irish baron of some fifty years ago and Marjory was to be attired in the dress of an Irish baroness. Together Speed had pictured them being one of the hits of the Costume Ball. To begin with, Marjory's hair was of a color often attributed to the Irish—red. But it was an attractive shade of red which many preferred to call auburn. And Marjory, dressed as a baroness of old Ireland would easily pass for a maid of Erin.

"If we don't win the prize," Speed had told himself, "We should come close to it!"

His departure for the Ball, therefore, was made in high spirits. It was nice of his father to let him have the car for the evening. He did not particularly care to be seen on the city streets clothed as he was. The bright green costume would look out of place anywhere but the ball-room floor. That part of it might be concealed, Speed had slipped on his long overcoat though the evening was warm enough to have done without it.

"Look out, guys! Here he comes!" whispered a stoutly built figure crouching behind the hedge at the Coulter home as an automobile came to a stop out in front. A line of figures suddenly became breathlessly silent, eyes on their leader who was stationed where he could peer through the hedge and give the signal when the right moment was at hand for them to jump out.

The occupant of the car stepped gayly from his machine and hurried in the entrance to the Coulter home, whistling softly.

"Pssst!" sounded the signal.

And, as the caller on Marjory Coulter passed the hedge, a cloud of black forms descended upon him so suddenly that there was no time for an outcry, whisking him off his feet and sweeping him around the house, through the backyard and into the alley with bewildering swiftness.

"Great work, gang!" congratulated their ringleader, as the kidnapped North Sider was pushed into another automobile. "Climb on the running boards if you can't get in. We'll get this baby to headquarters and then the circus'll begin!"

CHAPTER II

BIMBO'S TORTURE CHAMBER

"LET me go, you guys!" pleaded a muffled voice during the ride through South Oakland streets and alleys to the secret rendezvous of the South Side gang.

"We'll let you go!" was the answer. "When we get good and ready!"

"This is no fair!" protested a greatly agitated Speed Durgan. "You can't pick on a fellow when he's going to call on a girl! Look out for this costume, too. I just rented it!"

"Then we'll rent it some more!" jeered Sam, Bimbo's trusted lieutenant. With that he took out a handkerchief and tore it in the darkness so that it made a ripping sound.

"You'll pay for this!" cried the victim, struggling to get free. "You can't tear my costume and get away with it!"

"Hey! Aren't you supposed to be Irish?" taunted Kinky. "Can't you take a joke?"

"This is no joke!" rejoined Speed, feelingly. "And you fellows will find it out soon enough!

I'm supposed to be at the party by nine o'clock . . ."

"Sorry—but you're going to be a trifle late!"

"What's Marjory going to think—seeing my car outside and me nowhere around?"

The South Side gang roared.

"She's probably going to think you're absent-minded," joshed Bimbo, who had been too busy driving the car to take much part in the twit-ting. "I thought you'd learned your little lesson, Speed, that you're not wanted on this side of town!"

"This is a free country . . . !" Speed objected. "I . . . !"

"It may be a free country but it's not a free city. You come over here at your own risk. We told you that before—when we made you walk the plank!"

Another roar from the gang. Though it was dark and, perhaps fortunately, could not be seen, Speed's face turned red. Would they never get done kidding him about that? But what did they intend doing to him tonight? In all prob-ability it would be something more severe since the other lesson had apparently not soaked in.

"Where you taking me?" Speed gasped, as the car came to a stop.

"Wouldn't you like to know?" rasped Bimbo. "Keep that gunny sack over his head, gang. All right, North Sider, get out of the car and stretch those weak knees of yours!"

Speed had stumbled in trying to follow orders, as though his knees had given way beneath him.

"Listen, fellows—you want to think what you're doing! You're apt to get in trouble over this!"

"Now that's thoughtful of you to be so considerate of us, Mr. Durgan!" replied Sam, in sugar sweet tones. "But don't you worry one bit—unless it's about yourself."

The kidnapped youth was led up an embankment, Bimbo lighting the way with a flashlight.

"Duck your head!" he was commanded, as entrance to the hangout under the big warehouse was made.

A shack had been built with spare boards and parts of dry goods boxes with sections of the steel framework under the building serving as the boundary. Into this shack the blindfolded

Speed Durgan was led. Bimbo quickly touched a match to some candles and seated himself in the elevated chair reserved for the Chief.

"All right—let the prisoner see!" he commanded.

The gunny sack was jerked off the captive's head and Speed blinked dazedly as he looked about in the flickering candle light. A skull and cross bones had been painted in red over the head of the Chief who appeared prodigious in size as he stared down at the prisoner before him.

"Well, Speed, what have you got to say for yourself?" snapped the leader of the South Side gang.

"I think you're a bum!" was the defiant retort of the leader of the North Side crowd.

"Enter that statement in the court record!" Bimbo gravely directed.

His lieutenant, Sam Wade, made an elaborate pretense at scribbling in a notebook.

"And put a black mark against it!" Bimbo added. Then, turning to the captive: "Anything else?"

"Yes," said Speed. "It's five minutes after nine. Marjory will be wondering what's happened . . ."

"Not half as much as you're probably wondering what's *going* to happen!" suggested Bimbo, with a meaningful smile.

"See here, Bimbo! You've gone about far enough! I've heard you've been laying for me. But what have I done? We haven't pulled anything against you fellows since . . ."

"Since you rotten egged us after the football game last fall!" charged Bimbo. "Phooey I can smell those eggs yet! No, you haven't pulled anything since but the memory lingers on. And you're going to pay for that little party, old boy!"

"You bet he's going to pay!" chorused the gang.

"I didn't think of the rotten egg idea!" protested Speed.

"No, but you certainly helped carry it out!" rejoined Bimbo. "That old pitching arm of yours whizzed eggs at us like streaks."

Speed grinned, nervously. "Some of the eggs *were* streaks," he admitted. "They broke as they left my hand. We suffered about as much as you did!"

"Not by a darned sight!" ranted Bimbo. "One of your pitches caught me in the back of the neck and ruined a suit of winter underwear. Why wouldn't I be laying for you? Even the hens should be laying for you after that!"

Speed was silent. He didn't know quite how to take the physically powerful Bimbo. Apparently the South Side Chieftain had a sense of humor but preferred to joke rather than be joked with. That Bimbo would release him without imposing some personal discomfiture was doubtful. The opportunity for revenge was too good. If tables were reversed, Speed knew that he would be for giving Bimbo a dose of his own medicine. That is, did he not fear later retaliation . . . the sort of retaliation which was apt to be meted out to him any moment.

"Can't we come to some understanding?" Speed appealed. "What's the use of North and South scrapping all the time? Let's bury the hatchet!"

"Can't do that," replied Bimbo, airily. "We've no hatchet to bury. And we wouldn't bury it if we did have. You and your gang just don't mix with us. You're okay on your side the river but when you come over here you're all wet!"

"I wasn't bothering you fellows," defended

Speed. "I was on my way to a party. If you'd let me alone . . . !"

"Only on one condition!" countered Bimbo.

"And what's that?" demanded Speed.

"That you quit calling on Marjory!"

Speed's mouth opened wide as he gazed up at his stocky rival.

"You—you're kidding?" he finally managed.

"All right, if you think so!" was Bimbo's answer. "The girls on this side of town go with the fellows on this side of town. That's an unwritten law and if you don't know it by this time, you ought to be finding it out!"

"Why, that—that's ridiculous!" stammered Speed. "Why, I . . . why, Marjory used to live next door to us. She and I . . . er . . . we're the best of friends and . . . !"

"The best of friends must part!" declared Bimbo, reminiscent of something he had heard, but which, nevertheless, had a majestic ring to it.

"You can't do that!" objected Speed. "You can't bust up friendships! I'll go calling on Marjory as much as I please . . . and you just try to stop me!"

"We *have* stopped you, haven't we?" grinned

Bimbo. "You went calling on her tonight—and what happened? It's just going to be too bad for you, Speed, but if you're going to hold out like this, you've got to take the consequences!"

"I'll have you guys arrested!" threatened the leader of the North Side crowd. "I'll find out where this place is you've brought me to and I'll . . . !"

"Here's your last chance!" broke in Bimbo. "You going to do what we tell you or aren't you?"

Speed glanced about at the enemy faces surrounding him. He was hopelessly outnumbered, a prisoner in the South Side's stronghold. No telling what they might have in mind doing to him. Anything very disturbing would ruin his evening. The Costume Ball was quite the event of the season in North Oakland. How could he bear to miss it? And this Irish costume which he'd paid five hard-earned dollars to rent for the occasion!

"You know what I have a notion to do?" proposed Bimbo, suddenly. "Put on this funny green suit and take Marjory to the party myself!"

The gang laughed at the suggestion but Speed squirmed uneasily.

"Hands off!" he ordered. "The suit's not mine. I . . . !"

"Off with his coat!" commanded the South Side leader.

Speed was seized and, though he resisted strenuously, his coat was jerked off, revealing him just as he was dressed for the Ball.

"Very cute!" approved Lieutenant Sam Wade, dryly. "Want the outfit, Bimbo?"

"No," decided the Chieftain. "I'm afraid it wouldn't fit me. But that color gives me an idea. We've got a swell shade of green in that paint can over there. Came from your father's store, too," he added, with a nod at Speed.

"Here's the can." presented Sam. "There's a couple more—of red and blue."

"Good! Let's have 'em!" said Bimbo. "And that old paint brush the men on this job threw away. Also that old pair of paint-spotted overalls!"

"What you going to do?" demanded Speed, wide-eyed.

"Nothing much," replied Bimbo, mischievously. "Just try some of your Dad's paints out on you!"

"No! No!" objected Speed. "Listen to me a minute, you fellows! I'm half an hour late to the Ball right now and I won't be able to go at all if . . . !"

"Put those overalls on him!" directed Bimbo, taking the paint brush and stirring it around in the cans.

"Those dirty overalls!" cried Speed. "Have a heart! They won't go on over this costume! Hey! Let go my legs . . .!"

"Who said they wouldn't go on?" grinned Bimbo, a minute later, having held Speed while two of his accomplices did the job. Now you're beginning to look like your father's son—and when you get these dabs of paint on your face and hands . . .!"

"I'll get you for this!" fumed the leader of the North Side crowd.

"But just now we've got *you!*" Sam reminded. "Which can of paint do you want to use on him first, Bimbo?"

"The green since it's St. Patrick's day!" specified the South Side chieftain. "Now hold him, gang! I'm particular about how I smear this on his face!"

"You'd better be!" shouted Speed. "You'd better not put it on at all!"

"This is Paint Up week!" declared Bimbo, lifting a dripping paint brush from the can of green paint. "I'm sure your father wouldn't object to this! Just a little sample of his products where all the folks can see it! Now, I'd advise you not to move your head as I don't imagine you would like to get any of this paint in your hair."

"I'll say I wouldn't!" replied an agonized Speed Durgan. "This paint is the very dickens to get off! I painted the house last year and I . . . ! See here, Bimbo! . . . Hey! Look out for my eyes!"

"Then hold still!. . . I can't promise anything artistic unless you hold still. I dipped into your left eyebrow there. Sorry but you moved at the wrong time. You'd be surprised how green becomes you! . . . Now, Sam—let's have the red can. His cheeks look pale."

"Great grief!" moaned Speed, "This is terrible!"

"How do you know? you can't see yourself! It's really improving your looks. Giving you a little real color!"

Bimbo smacked Speed's cheeks with the brush, leaving great splotches of red.

"This an outrage!" declared the victim, more resigned to his fate since there appeared to be nothing he could do about it.

"Feeling *blue?*" teased Bimbo. "Well, here's some blue to go with it . . . and I think blue ears would look pretty!"

No sooner said than done. Speed's ears became bright blue in color, completing a rather ghastly if not clownish facial appearance. A green forehead, red cheeks and blue ears.

"The man from Mars!" exclaimed Kinky, and the gang howled.

"I can't go to the Ball now!" moaned the leader of the North Side crowd. "It'll take me weeks to get this paint off!"

"Naw, nothing like that!" reassured Bimbo. "Just buy a can of your Dad's paint remover! Here—hold out your hands while we touch them up a bit!"

"The North American Indian!" pronounced

Sam, when Bimbo had finished. "How ferocious he looks. See him show his teeth, gang! Watch out—he's apt to bite!"

The victim, with arms and legs being tightly held, could only glare up at his captors, the whites of his eyes weird in the candle light.

"How do you like our little Torture Chamber?" inquired Al Cort, another gang member. "Wouldn't you like to visit us again sometime?"

"I'll get even with you fellows if it's the last thing I do!" Speed answered.

"Yeah—I suppose you'll beat us in baseball for this?" guyed Bimbo.

"We'll do that anyway!" said Speed. "You fellows were lucky to win the last two years. If I have anything to say about it, there won't any of you reach first base!"

"No, I suppose not," acknowledged Bimbo, ruefully. "I'm not interested in first base so that let's me out. All I'm interested in is home plate and, boy, I can hit you for a homer any day you walk out on the mound!"

"You just think you can, because you happened to connect on a couple of balls you shouldn't have hit!"

"That so? I've spoiled a perfect season for you twice and I'm going to do it again. Your brand of pitching is pie for me!" declared Bimbo, cockily. "I've got your number and you know it!"

Speed made no reply to this. Instead he put forth a sudden effort to free himself.

"Getting anxious to call on Marjory? Well, we'll let you go in just a minute. But first we want to hang a little sign on your back!"

"Now what?" groaned the captive, miserably.

For answer, Bimbo produced a placard which had been taken from a street corner. It bore the printed words:

BEAUTIFY YOUR CITY
PAINT UP
and
CLEAN UP!

"We ought to drop him off in the heart of the business district!" suggested Sam, when the placard had been tied in place. "He'd make a great walking advertisement for his Dad's store!"

"That's a good idea," Bimbo chuckled. "But

I'd rather drop him off at Marjory's this way. I think she'd get a big kick out of his make-up."

"I don't want to see Marjory this way!" begged Speed. "You let me off near home. I'll send Dad over for the car!"

"Us go over on the North side of town?" said Bimbo. "Not on your life! You really look great, Speed, old man! Just tell Marjory you're late because it took you so long to get fixed up!"

"I won't tell her anything of the kind. I'll tell her . . . !"

"Put the gunny sack over his head!" ordered Bimbo. "We're taking him for another ride!"

Led down the same embankment he had been helped up, Speed wondered where it could be that they had taken him. He counted his footsteps as he was led down to the car. Exactly sixty-two! If he could only figure out the hiding place! But he did not dare attempt to remove the gunny sack from his head and, even had he dared, his captors were holding him too firmly to permit it. The humiliation of facing Marjory in this condition now impressed itself upon him. Quite possibly she may have noticed his car out in front and spread an alarm. The police might even be on the lookout for him. Certainly Marjory would be unable to explain the presence of his car and his mysterious absence. Speed had a sudden surge of hope that the officers might be laying in ambush and pounce out upon this South Side gang as they stopped to push him out near the Coulter residence.

"It would serve 'em right!" he told himself, bitterly. "They've spoiled my evening and heaven only knows when I'll be able to look natural again!"

"There's still more paint left if you decide to visit Marjory again," reminded Bimbo as the car approached Speed's getting out place. "So let this be a warning to you!"

The gunny sack was removed and Speed saw that Bimbo was about to turn onto the street where Marjory lived.

"Hold on, there, Bimbo!" shouted Sam, looking ahead. "Who's that by Speed's car? Good gosh! Don't turn down that street! There's a copper!"

"Let's put Speed out right here!" said Kinky.

"Okay!" agreed Bimbo, considerably sobered

by sight of the police. "Push him out, guys! And don't you squeal on us, North Sider, or it's going to be just too bad for you!"

Speed Durgan, helped out by many hands, landed in the grass between curb and sidewalk as the car slowed down to perhaps ten miles an hour. The highly colored figure picked himself up and shook his fist after the carload of kidnappers. It was just as he thought. The police had been notified. Marjory was greatly upset. And his father . . . !

"But I guess I'd better not yell for help!" Speed decided. "This is my affair. I've got to settle this score some other way!"

And so Bimbo and his followers put on speed and whizzed away while a dejected young fellow turned his steps toward the Coulter house, wondering how such a strange spectacle as he now presented would be received.

CHAPTER III

AN UNEXPECTED DEVELOPMENT

"Speed! Good gracious! Is this really you?"

Marjory, attired as an Irish baroness but now quite unmindful of the fact, was on the porch as a sorry looking figure turned in at the hedge.

"It's me," answered a familiar voice, in an attempt to be reassuring. "Awfully sorry I had to be so late!"

"What on earth happened?" cried Marjory, concernedly, as her intended escort reached the porch and sank down on the steps. "What are you doing in such an outlandish get-up—and your hands and face . . . ? Speed Durgan— you're a sight!"

Policeman Tracy who had been called to the scene of the strange disappearance, strode up from having taken down the license number of the car and other data.

"Is this the bird who was supposed to be missing?" he asked of Marjory.

"Oh, yes, officer!" replied the girl who had formerly lived on the North Side. "I—I guess everything's all right now, thank you!"

"I don't know as it is!" returned the policeman, eyeing Speed shrewdly. "What happened to you, young fellah?"

"I . . . er . . . a . . . I was taken for a ride," Speed answered, and managed a weak grin.

"It looks like you were taken for more than that!" was the policeman's observation. "Who did this?"

"I—I'd rather not say," replied Speed.

"Where do you live?" demanded the patrolman.

"North Side," said Speed.

"Oh, well that explains a lot," was the blue coat's rejoinder. "So you don't want to press charges, eh?"

Speed shook his head and the copper grinned.

"Okay! Here's wishing you luck. Looks like you've got a long way to go to get even!"

"I'll get even—don't worry!" vowed Speed, with a glance at Marjory. And, as the policeman took his departure, he asked of her, anxiously: "Did you call my folks? Does Dad know . . . ?"

"I was just about to call," Marjory answered.

"It gave me a terrible fright. My folks were out and I was here all alone. I couldn't believe it was your car out in front at first. I thought you were just late. But, finally, I thought I'd better investigate. When I found it *was* your car I was naturally excited and I spoke to the policeman who was passing. He said it was probably a prank of some kind and he was just examining the car when you came up. I'd have phoned your folks in another minute."

"Then I'm glad I got here when I did," said Speed, greatly relieved. "And maybe you'll let me clean up in your house? I'd rather Dad didn't know about this. He'd be for causing these fellows trouble. Do you know if you've got some turpentine?"

"Come inside where I can get a good look at you," invited Marjory.

Speed followed with obvious reluctance. But what else was there for him to do?

On getting him under a light, Marjory had him turn about so that she could see him from all sides and then she burst into a fit of laughter.

"Speed—I hope you'll forgive me—But you're the funniest thing I ever looked at!"

"Well, if you can just show me to the turpentine, I'll . . . !"

"No, no! Let the paint stay on—for tonight! They've fixed you up grand. Those overalls, that sign and all! . . . It gives me a fine idea! I'll have to change my own looks to match!"

"Wh-wh-what do you m-mean?" stammered Speed, in shocked surprise. "Y-you don't intend for me to go to the—the Costume Ball like this, d-do you?"

"Why not?" retorted Marjory, gleefully.

"This 'paint up and clean up' idea is very timely. It might make a hit! You wait here and I'll make myself ready."

"But, I . . . !" Speed started to protest.

Marjory, however, had hurried from the room. He stood staring after her a moment and mumbling to himself.

"She must be crazy. I can't go to the Ball. They'd laugh me off the floor."

There was a full length mirror in the vestibule. Speed edged toward it, impelled by curiosity. What did he really look like? It must be pretty terrible. Worse than a comic character in a funny paper. And here he'd planned for Marjory and himself to be quite the swellest looking couple on the floor! Chances were, Marjory was merely trying to make the best of it. She was a mighty good sport and . . . !

"Great suffering cats!" exclaimed Speed, as he caught sight of his image in the glass. "I don't wonder Marj laughed. My looks would stop a train. No, they would run a train off the track! If I didn't know this was myself I'd think it was somebody else! But I never saw anybody else like I look and nobody else ever did either. Gee, this paint looks like it's on to stay . . . and the longer I leave it on the harder it'll be to get off. But if Marjory's . . ."

"Here I am!" announced a voice. "Now, what do you think of me?"

Speed swung about and stood staring. The transition was startling. From an Irish baroness who had looked charming enough to rule old Erin, Marjory had converted herself into an Irish scrubwoman. There were plentiful smudges of charcoal on her face, her hair was straggly and unkempt, and she wore a torn and patched old dress over her green costume. As a final touch, Marjory was carrying a mop and pail.

"Great!" exclaimed Speed, his dejection vanishing as he realized what Marjory had in mind. "We're the 'Paint Up and Clean Up' twins. Come on—we're an hour late to the Ball but maybe it's all the better. They'll be sure to notice us when we come in!"

With this, Speed gave Marjory his arm and conducted her from the house to his car in stately fashion. Several passersby stopped to stare in open-mouthed amazement and rub hands before their eyes as if they thought they were seeing things.

"It was Bimbo Bailey who did this to you, wasn't it?" Marjory asked, as Speed drove off.

"Well, I . . . er . . ." said Speed. "I suppose that wouldn't be hard to guess."

"No," Marjory smiled. "Especially since Bimbo wanted to take me to the picture show to-night."

"He *did?*" Speed almost swerved into a traffic tower. "He's got a lot of crust!"

"Oh, I don't know. I think he's an interesting fellow," mused Marjory. "I may go out with him some time."

"*What?*"

"Speed! Be careful—you almost hit that milk wagon!"

"Say —don't you start kidding me! I've gone through enough tonight. You don't want to have anything to do with that guy. Of course you can't help your folks moving over on the South Side but you don't have to go with . . . !"

"I'm curious to see what Bimbo's really like," said Marjory, frankly. "He does some crazy things, I'll admit, but then—so do you fellows That rotten egg business . . . !"

Speed's face flushed. "We wouldn't pull anything if they didn't. We can't let Bimbo and his bunch step all over us! They're plotting something all the time. I'll bet Bimbo wouldn't want to be taking you to a picture show if it wasn't for the fact that I am going with you!"

Marjory laughed. "Now do you think that last remark is very complimentary to me?"

"Aw, I didn't mean it that way. I'm sorry, Marj! I'm just upset about this whole affair. Say—here's an idea! Let him take you to a picture show if he asks you again and find out from him, if you can, where he and his gang have their hangout!"

Marjory looked at Speed. "Is that where you were taken tonight?"

"Yes—with a gunny sack over my head. I couldn't tell where I was. Might have been along the river bank somewhere. I had to climb quite a slope after they took me from the car."

"What would you do if you knew where the hangout was?"

"Why, I—I'd lead our gang to it and wreck the place!" declared Speed.

"And start another chain of vengeance!" predicted Marjory. "No, Speed, I can't play the spy. I hope I may be trusted by both sides."

"You know what they say?" reminded Speed. "Once a North Sider, always a North Sider! And that goes for South Siders, too!"

They were crossing the bridge over the Kent river with the lights of both sides of town blinking at them.

"Nevertheless," insisted Marjory, mischievously. "I'm going to try to be as neutral as this bridge!"

Merry makers at the St. Patrick's Costume Ball who knew and had been expecting Marjory and Speed could not imagine what was keeping them. Salty Peters, Teaser Burke and Floyd Tenney, gathering in a nook near the ballroom floor, talked the matter over.

"I told Speed to look out for Bimbo," said Salty. "Do you suppose he's been waylaid?"

"Don't know," rejoined Teaser. "I'm glad my girl doesn't live in South Side. I learned my little lesson last year. You'll never catch me alone over there after dark!"

He grinned as he spoke but his remark was half-serious. Anyone who had encountered the might of Bimbo and his gang felt the same way.

"He should have had a body guard with him to go over and get Marjory!" opined Floyd.

"Of course his car might have broken down or he could have blown a tire," reflected Salty. "But somehow I've a hunch that something else has happened."

"Well, we can't do anything about it now, if it has," declared Teaser. "I'm sorry I made my dance program up with him before the Ball. Ruth likes to dance with Speed but we've passed her dance with him and I haven't another dance spot open."

"Never mind," consoled Floyd. "Maybe

when Speed gets here he won't feel like dancing anyway. If he's had a run-in with Bimbo he may be carried in here on a stretcher."

"I wonder if we shouldn't call the hospital?" suggested Salty, dryly. "No kidding, guys— I think Speed's scared to death of Bimbo. I had a little talk with him late this afternoon. At first I only thought Bimbo had Speed's number in baseball . ... . but I guess he's got it all around."

"Whose number hasn't he got? Tell me that!" defied Floyd. "South Side's ruling us right now and they have been since Bimbo's come into power. I think . . ."

A gale of laughter, sweeping the ballroom, interrupted Floyd's remarks and caused the three youths to look at one another wonderingly.

"What's up?" asked Salty.

"Something funny must have happened," decided Teaser.

Together the three stepped into the ballroom to see the dancers making way for a strange couple who were meeting with a riotous reception.

"Look at that!" cried Salty. "Boy, if that's

not clever! . . . A new kind of Gold Dust twins!"

"See the sign on that guy's back—'Paint Up and Clean Up'!" read Floyd. "Why didn't we think of something like that? And those overalls! They're so covered with paint they look like they could stand alone!"

"The girl looks just as bad!" observed Teaser. "Say—the trouble they must have gone to for that get-up! They ought to win the prize hands down!"

"The judges are sure giving 'em the once over!" said Floyd, pointing to the judges' box.

"Holy mackerel!" gasped Salty, in great excitement. "Take a good squint, you birds, and tell me—do my eyes deceive me? Aren't those two Marjory and Speed?"

Teaser and Floyd started and stared.

"Well, bowl me over with a feather!" swore Teaser. "Right you are!"

"Can you beat it?" exclaimed Floyd. "Hey, Speed!"

The couple were making a round of the ballroom amid laughter and applause. Hearing Floyd's summons they edged over.

"Howdee!" greeted Speed, from behind his paint-creased face.

"You're the hit of the evening!" shouted Salty above the din. "How'd you think this up, old man? I'll bet your Dad gave you the idea! It's a good piece of advertising for him! Everybody's talking . . . !"

"My Dad didn't have anything to do with it," rejoined Speed who was highly enjoying the ovation.

"Then it was Marjory!" divined Floyd, bowing before the Irish scrubwoman. "Speed couldn't have done it all himself! He's not that original!"

Marjory smiled, showing some teeth that had been blacked out. The dancers crowding about, screamed. A further commotion developed when Marjory set her mop pail down and removed the mop with a flourish.

"Hey! She's got real water in that pail!" someone shouted, and the dancers scattered.

"Why were you so late?" demanded Teaser. "We lost our dance with you!"

"Couldn't be helped," said Speed, tongue in his cheek. "It took us a long time to get fixed up."

"It sure must have!" agreed Salty, examining Speed closely. "Say, man, that's not real paint you've got on your face and hands, is it?"

Speed nodded, exchanging glances with a beaming Marjory.

"Good night! You'll never get that stuff off!"

"I don't care," was Speed's irresponsible answer. "This is worth it!"

"We take our hats off!" complimented Floyd. "Listen! . . . What's that? . . . They're calling you! They want you to go up on the platform. It's the judges! Oh, baby—it looks like you're going to be awarded the prize!"

On their way to the stage at one end of the ballroom, a deliriously happy couple consulted one another.

"Do you think we should tell how we came to carry out this idea?" asked Speed.

"By all means!" said Marjory. "I'd give Bimbo all the credit. He'll just love to hear that he's helped you win a hundred dollars!"

"*Won't* he?" laughed Speed, as he helped Marjory up the steps to the stage. "Say—I never even dreamed .. .. but what a revenge this is going to be!"

Amid tumultuous applause, the chairman of the judges presented a loving cup and one hundred dollars in gold to Marjory and Speed who accepted it graciously. Speed stuck the money in his pocket and patted it affectionately while Marjory brought further laughs by shaking her head despondently and returning to her mopping. The little ceremony over, Speed was finally compelled to respond to insistent demands for a speech.

"Folks, there's just one thing I'd like to say," he began. "You all know the rivalry that's on between the North and the South? Well, tonight I was caught by a South Side gang who smeared me with paint, thinking they'd keep me from the party. I probably wouldn't have gone, either, if it hadn't been for Miss Coulter but she seemed to think the paint improved my looks . . .!"

There were howls from the merry makers.

"She was right!" shouted someone.

Speed grinned. Nothing could affect his good humor now. He jingled the gold coins in his pocket.

"Miss Coulter and I," he concluded, "want to publicly thank Bimbo Bailey and his crowd for giving us the idea that won the prize. It was

very nice of them and we only hope I
mean . . . that is— *I* only hope—that I may
be able to return the favor some time—with
interest!"

This brought a roar from those in attendance
at the Costume Ball.

"Spoken like an Irishman!" called out a
staunch North Sider.

And the ballroom buzzed with amused comment as the dancing was resumed.

"You keep the silver cup," Speed insisted on
returning Marjory to her home following a
most enjoyable termination to an evening which
had started out disastrously. "And here's your
half of the hundred. Better sleep with it under
your pillow until you can get it safe in the bank.
I never had so much money at one time!"

Marjory smiled. "Good night, Speed! I've
had a perfectly thrilling time! I hope you're
able to get the paint off!"

"I'm not in a hurry now," rejoined the leader
of the North Side gang. "Looks like it's brought
me good luck. I may leave it on just to make
Bimbo mad every time he sees me! You're a
peach, Marj! You've helped me get even with
Bimbo and then some!"

CHAPTER IV

SPEED SAVES HIS FACE

MORNING papers, announcing the winners of the costume prize at the St. Patrick's Costume Ball held in North Oakland, carried humorous stories relating the manner in which Bob "Speed" Durgan, son of the man who owned the biggest paint store in town, had come by the make-up which won the favor of the judges.

"South Side Gang's Prank Becomes Boomerang!" the Morning Star declared in front page headlines, going on to state: "Bimbo Bailey, leader of South High's crowd, will probably think twice before trying to put one over upon Speed Durgan, rival leader of the North High boys, after last night's boomerang. Bimbo is wearing a long face today and Speed is wearing a painted but happy face as a result of the hazing he received which, all unintentionally, fixed him so that he could win the handsome prize offered by the Costume Ball committee for the most originally dressed and made up couple. Set upon as he was about to call for his partner,

Miss Marjory Coulter, of seven hundred Elm Street, South Oakland, Speed was carried off by the Bimbo crowd and smeared with paint from cans containing the labels of his father's store. A sign: 'Beautify Your City—Paint Up and Clean Up' was then hung on his back and Speed was returned to near the Coulter home where he was pushed out of the car. The hazers were confident that they had embarrassed their North Side rival beyond words and that they had made it impossible for him to attend the Ball with his lady friend. But Miss Coulter, enterprising young lady that she is, used her ingenuity to invent a character for herself in keeping with that which the gang had made out of her escort —and the result was so startling and so effective as to prove the unanimous choice of the judges. There is an old adage: 'he who has the last laugh, laughs hardest' and all North Oakland is laughing heartily today . . ."

"Horse shoes!" growled Bimbo, as he read the story in the presence of his gang.

"According to this we're entitled to part of the prize money!" grinned Sam. "We sure handed Speed a rabbit's foot without realizing it, all right! One hundred bucks he gets just because we muss him up with paint! Zowie!"

"And we'll never hear the last of it!" muttered Bimbo. "The razzing those North Siders will give us! What we should have done was to keep Speed kidnapped until the party was over!"

"Well, what we should have done won't do us any good now," said Kinky. "We had Speed pretty worried last night but this turning of the tables is apt to make him feel like he's sitting on top of the world. What we've got to do is fix him so that there's no come-back!"

"Right!" affirmed Bimbo, determinedly. "You know what I'd like to do this year? I'd like to drive that guy from the pitcher's box. It's the last crack we'll have at him and he naturally will be out to hang it on us since we've beat him out on a couple of close ones before!"

"Yeah—we beat him—but I'm not so sure we'd have done it if we hadn't gotten his goat!" replied Stub. "He's some sweet pitcher!"

"What's wrong with getting a guy's goat?" Bimbo demanded. "No law against it, is there? If a pitcher can't keep from getting rattled, that's his fault! I know Speed doesn't like to pitch to me . . . and, believe me, I'm going to let him know, every chance I get, that I know it! Way I feel now—I could hit him for a homer every time up!"

"We'll be satisfied if you hit him for one— like you've done before!" rejoined Al. "I think North's going to have the best nine they've ever had this season so it's going to be tougher for us to trim Speed."

"But it's *got* to be done!" declared Bimbo, and the word 'got' again had its magic affect. Heads nodded in unison.

"Yes, we gotta do it!" was the answering chorus.

Opening practice for North High was fraught with excitement and enthusiasm. Speed Durgan was quite the hero of the moment with tell-tale paint marks still on his ears, eyebrows and around the hair line.

"It's a good omen!" declared Hank Perry, veteran third baseman. "Speed's won his first victory over Bimbo—and it points to another victory for us when we play Bimbo and his bunch this year!"

"Here's hoping!" the other team members exclaimed, fervently. "If we win—we'll borrow a load of paint from Speed's Dad and paint the town red!"

"If we win, Dad'll give us all the paint we want!" grinned Speed. "He's so tickled over the advertising he got by my winning the Costume prize that he's sent one of his men up to paint our house and let me off the job!"

"I'll bet you appreciated that more than winning the hundred dollars," kidded Teaser.

"Almost!" Speed admitted, humorously.

Coach Fred Hart, beyond seeing to it that team candidates loosened up their arms and legs by throwing and running practice, did not try to put them through any paces. He was fortunately situated this season with practically a veteran nine—six positions already filled unless some candidates showed surprising ability to unseat former regulars.

"This year I hope we can attain an undefeated record," the Coach told team candidates at the close of the session. "We've just missed out two years in succession but this year, something tells me we're going to break the jinx

South High has held over us. It's ridiculous—winning over some of the best teams in the state and letting a nine with a much poorer season's record beat us out."

"You said it!" murmured Steve Clawson, veteran catcher, glaring at Speed who was staring down at the ground.

"The trouble has been that you fellows have tried to play South High instead of playing baseball," analyzed Coach Hart. "And you can't have your minds on that South Side bunch and put up a good game. That Bimbo, beyond being a corking ball player, is the best I ever saw at getting another fellow's goat! He'll pull almost anything that an umpire will let him get away with to attract your attention away from the game, being wise enough to know that then is when you're going to make an error or fail to do something you should have done! I'm telling you this at the very start this year so you won't have any alibi and so you'll train yourselves to guard against South High's system. Their theory is 'get your opponent's goat first and you've got the game!'"

"We learned our lesson last season!" declared Salty.

"*I* did, at any rate!" said Speed, soberly, recalling his wild pitch which had lost the contest.

"Well, if *you* did, that's the main thing!" said Steve, his battery mate, and laughed. "I broke all records in the high jump going after that pitch of yours but it was still three feet over my head!"

"Don't mention it!" begged Speed. "Give me a chance to live it down!"

"All will be forgiven if you help us win this year!" assured Teaser. "Bygones will be bygones!"

"We'll win!" said Speed, grimly. "It'll be our last game for most of us—and we've got to win—for North High!"

That word '*got*'—used, this time, by the opposite side! And, from the determination expressed by both Bimbo and Speed, it commenced to look very much like the case of an irresistible force being destined to meet up against an impenetrable object!

Weeks passed quickly—weeks of preparation on both sides of the Kent River. Rumor had it that South High had dug up a pitcher who would give North High's pitching ace, Speed Durgan, a terrific battle when the rival nines met. This pitcher's name was Ivan Siano but, after the first few scheduled games, his mound performance was such that all South Oakland took to calling him "Ivan, the Terrible."

"We've had to kid North High out of the games before," said one South rooter, "But we'll give them an argument this year without trying to get their goats! This boy Ivan will match Speed, pitch for pitch!"

Such declarations as this, traveling north across the river, caused North Oaklanders to wonder whether this "Ivan, the Terrible" was not another form of kidding that South High had developed in an attempt to break down their team's morale.

"Bimbo's doing most of his shooting at Speed Durgan!" figured a North High supporter. "And he knows, if Speed feels he's going to be up against a pitcher who's as good as he is, plus having to face the fence-busting Bimbo—that he's going to have his hands full winning. You've got to discount the reports about this Ivan person at least fifty percent! He's won the first few games this season but that doesn't necessarily mean he's in Speed's class."

"In other words," joshed a second supporter. "This Ivan's not as hot as he's painted!"

" 'Painted' is right!" acknowledged the first supporter, with a grin. "That's all those South Siders do—they highly color everything!"

Waynesboro High was scheduled to meet North and South Oakland High Schools on consecutive Saturdays. It was the only school to play both Oakland nines and fans looked ahead to Waynesboro's encounters as a means of determining the relative strength of the rival local teams.

"We can tell pretty accurately, after the Waynesboro games, how good this pitcher, Ivan Siano, really is—and how he stacks up as compared to Speed," said a rooter.

"We've one good break anyway," pointed out another. "North High has an open date the Saturday that Bimbo and his bunch tackle Waynesboro, which ought to give our boys a chance to look this Ivan, the Terrible over. That is—if they dare go over to South Side's ball yard!"

"Which is a question," was the rejoinder. "Neither side welcomes scouting and if they spotted a rival in the stands they'd probably find a way to make it hot for him!"

But in this supposition, insofar as South High was concerned, the rooter was wrong. In fact, Bimbo Bailey, having finally secured Marjory's consent to take her to a picture show, even ventured to suggest that she invite Speed Durgan over to see South's new pitching find hurl against Waynesboro.

"I think Speed would like to look Ivan over," said Bimbo. "And I want him to put his peepers on a fellow whom I think can really pitch!"

"Meaning by that, you don't think Speed is much of a pitcher himself?" asked the girl who had formerly lived on the North side.

"Oh, he manages to get by but he's soft picking for me. I murder his stuff! The other guys seem to have a little trouble on account of his change of pace—but I think they'll catch on this year. It's just a matter of proper timing . . . and we'll knock your friend from the wrong side of town out of the box!"

Bimbo grinned as he said this so Marjory

could not take offense. In fact she was just thinking to herself that Bimbo, as she had imagined, was really a very nice fellow. He was headstrong, perhaps; used to having his own way; enjoyed 'deviling' people and trying to get them upset; but, underneath it all, was the desire and intent to be a good sportsman. In taking the attitude he did toward North High he was simply following tradition. His pranks, sometimes executed with poor judgment, were threatening gestures of a leader who sought to maintain a reign of terror in name rather than practice. That he went too far, on occasion, was due to an excess of exuberance.

"I should think you'd be pretty careful what you tried to do to Speed from now on," teased Marjory. "After the way you helped him win a hundred dollars!"

"You got fifty of it, didn't you?" retorted Bimbo. "If you didn't, Speed gets another coating of paint that he won't win a prize on!"

"Yes, I received fifty dollars, thank you," assured Marjory, mischievously. "That's one reason I accepted your invitation to the show. I wanted to thank you personally for . . . ."

"Keep the change!" interrupted Bimbo, with a magnanimous wave of his hand. "That's the only part about the deal that made me feel good —thinking that half this award was coming to you! Say, I've got to give you credit for making something out of nothing! Speed looked like a wreck when we got through with him and if you hadn't figured how to cash in on his looks—I'll bet he wouldn't even have gone to the party!"

Marjory's face colored. "Oh, yes he would!" she insisted. "It would have taken more than what you did to stop Speed. He . . . .!"

Bimbo laughed.

"Don't you suppose I know that guy? You want the real low-down on Speed? I don't mean to hurt your feelings or anything but you get Speed in a tight spot and he just lacks nerve!"

"That's not so!" defended Marjory, loyally.

"No? What do you suppose made him walk me with the bases full year before last to force in the run that won the game for us? And what do you suppose made him uncork a wild pitch last year that threw the game away? Both accidents? Not on your life! Didn't see him do that in any other games, did you? I've just discovered his weakness and I work on it!"

"That's absurd!" Marjory still refused to believe. "Speed will show you this year. He . . .!"

"We'll beat him every time out!" declared Bimbo, with conviction.

"By fair means or foul!" twitted Marjory.

"Nothing unfair about taking advantage of a guy's weakness! That's strategy!" rejoined Bimbo. "Every team does that. Take football, for instance—the minute they discover a weak spot in the line they send the plays through it. There's ways of pulling the same stuff in baseball."

"Well, I'll just make you a good-natured bet that Speed beats you this time, no matter what you try to do to him," declared Marjory, spiritedly.

"What'll you bet?" Bimbo demanded, taking quick advantage of her offer. "Will you go to the South High party we always hold after the annual battle with North, if we win?"

"North has an annual party the same night," Marjory reminded, thinking of Speed and how he had taken her to this event the past two years.

"I know that!" grinned Bimbo. "But you're so sure North's going to win . . . that Speed's going to come through—why should you worry about not going to the north side doings with Speed? Of course, if we *should* happen to beat him, you'd be going with me instead of Speed and, what's more, you'd be staying on this side of town . . . which you ought to be doing anyhow!"

"I refuse to be put down as a one-sided girl!" laughed Marjory. "But I said I'd bet you and I'll take this wager. Next time I see Speed I'll tell him the arrangement."

"And tell him for me, if he'd like to come over and scout the Waynesboro team and get a load of our Ivan, the Terrible's pitching to come ahead and we'll keep hands off him! You'll have to give him this message or you'll never get him over here to see the game."

"How do I know but what you're angling for a truce?" kidded Marjory. "Hoping that the North Side will invite you over to see them play Waynesboro the week before—and guarantee to keep from doing anything to you?"

Bimbo gestured scornfully. "Naw! South doesn't have to scout North! We know what they've got. They can't spring any surprises on us!"

North High's game with Waynesboro, some weeks later, emphasized one of two things. Either Waynesboro had a stronger nine than it customarily put on the field, or Speed Durgan's pitching was not up to the form he was capable of showing. True, Speed had carried his team along to an unbroken string of victories and some of his admirers claimed for him that he was only as good as he had to be to win. But the fact remained that Waynesboro touched him for an even dozen hits and five runs, against seven runs for North High on nine hits and two very helpful errors.

"Not so hot!" was the opinion of South High fans who had watched the outcome of this game with interest. "Now we'll see what Ivan, the Terrible is able to do to that Waynesboro bunch next Saturday!"

"Are you coming over to our game?" Marjory asked Speed after witnessing North's defeat of Waynesboro.

"I . . . er . . . don't think so," was Speed's reply. "Why should I?"

"Bimbo thinks you should," said Marjory, eyeing Speed closely. "In fact, he told me to invite you."

"Oh, he did, did he? Wasn't that nice of him? Probably laying for me with another can of my Dad's paint!" Speed grinned.

"No," laughed Marjory. "He's promised not to touch you."

"I know his kind of promises!"

"But wouldn't you like to get a line on our pitching sensation?"

"Well, I suppose some of our fans will cover the game and give us a report."

"Listen, Speed!" spoke Marjory, determinedly. "I want you to come to South's game against Waynesboro with me!"

Speed looked his surprise.

"That sounds like a command."

"It is!" rejoined Marjory, feelingly. "Bimbo's said some unkind things about you and I want to prove to him that he's wrong."

"For instance?" asked Speed, face coloring.

"He implied that you were afraid of him,"

related Marjory. "And then he—he said you lacked *nerve!*"

Speed started. "But, you—you don't believe that?"

"I certainly don't. I even bet with Bimbo that you'd beat him this year."

"You did? What did you bet?"

"I bet the party you usually take me to against the party Bimbo wants to take me to," replied Marjory. "Both are on the same night, as you know, so it's up to you to win if . . .!"

"What in the world did you do that for?" cried Speed, obviously upset. "That's another slick one that Bimbo's pulled! He's always trying to get my goat. He made you that proposition, didn't he? You know, Marj, it's understood between us that this annual party is a yearly affair with us. Of course we . . . er . . .. I expect to beat South this year but it's foolish to make a bet like that. I'd call it off!"

"I can't do it!" said Marjory, decidedly. "It's a matter of honor with me, Speed. I was being taunted about you and I accepted the bet to show my faith in you. Now if you don't go out there and uphold that faith . . . !"

"I'll do my best, naturally. Just like I've done the past two years . . . but the breaks . . . ."

"Shall I tell Bimbo that you're coming over to see the game next Saturday?"

Speed hesitated. "I think he's cooking up a trap for me," he said, somewhat lamely. "He told me he'd fix me if he ever caught me on the South Side with you again. But, I . . . er . . . of course, that didn't mean anything to me. Just the same . . ."

"Speed Durgan!" addressed Marjory, discerningly. "I'm beginning to think . . . !"

"What time do you want me to call for you?" rejoined Speed, in an attempt to counteract her impression.

"Why, the game starts at two-thirty."

"Well, is two o'clock time enough?"

"That's fine," smiled Marjory.

"Tell Bimbo, if he really means what he says, to see that we get seats behind the plate so I can look this Ivan, the Terrible over right!" said Speed, emboldened now that he had made up his mind to go. "Maybe I can discover Bimbo's batting weakness, too! That is—if he has any!"

CHAPTER V

AN IMPORTANT DISCOVERY

"Lay off Speed," Bimbo told his followers the next Saturday afternoon when the rival pitcher was sighted in the stands behind home plate. "I arranged with Marj to get him over here. And get this, Ivan—give Waynesboro everything you've got today. I know you won't have to do it to win but I want Speed to soak up an eyeful of what you can do when you bear down!"

The dark skinned, dark-eyed Italian, son of a South Side cobbler, who had yet to taste defeat on the mound, grinned and nodded.

"You bet I'll bear down!" he said. "If I can't do better against this team than Speed did, I'll swallow a baseball. He'll see something today that'll make him lie awake nights!"

As it turned out, one Speed Durgan saw several things the very first inning which made him shudder. He saw the much discussed Ivan Siano strike out the first two Waynesboro batters and force the third to pop out to shortstop.

"He's got something," Speed told Marjory.

"A fast ball with a hop on it, mostly. He has very good control of it, which is the main thing. Seems to me he's started out pretty strong. We'll see how long he can keep this up!"

In the last half of the first inning, Speed also saw the mighty Bimbo stride to the plate with two out and a man on second and clout the first pitched ball over the centerfield fence for a home run. As Bimbo came trotting across the home plate, he deliberately doffed his cap and bowed to Speed.

"Just for your entertainment, old boy!" he called, and a partisan South High crowd roared while the fellow from North High became red of face.

"You didn't discover any weakness that time at bat, did you?" asked Marjory, enjoying Speed's temporary discomfiture.

"Not exactly," Speed admitted, smiling. "How that guy lands on the ball! I'll have to give him credit!"

Throughout the game Speed kept a wary eye on South High fellows about him, recognizing a few who had assisted in his capture the night of the widely heralded Costume Ball incident.

These followers of Bimbo returned his glances none too cordially, Speed thought, and his uneasiness grew as the game drew near a close. It seemed incredible that Bimbo's gang members didn't have something up their sleeves. But as much as he had loathed to visit their ball park, he had loathed admitting to Marjory that he actually feared coming. He couldn't ever admit to her that he feared anything . . . or anybody. It wouldn't do for him to admit to the fellows on his side of town, who had chosen him as their leader, that he actually feared Bimbo. All the North High crowd held Bimbo and his gang in awesome respect but even this was different than downright fear. And Speed, as he fidgeted in his seat, hoped ardently that he had not already betrayed his real feelings, either to his own followers . . . or to Marjory.

"It's foolish for me to let myself be affected this way," Speed tried to tell himself. "Nothing serious has ever happened to any fellow as a result of this feud . . . and the chances are that nothing will! So why should I worry?"

"What do you think of our pitcher, Siano?" a fan called to him.

The question brought Speed to attention with a start.

"He's fair," he replied, sparingly, in the face of Ivan's having pitched an amazing two-hit and no-run game up to the eighth inning.

"*Fair?*" laughed a fan, as those near Speed joined in. "He's pitching rings around you against the same team! I'd say he's darn *good!*"

"Waynesboro's got two big innings left!" grinned Speed. "They may get to him yet. Wait till after the game's over and I'll tell you how good he is!"

This remark drew fire upon Speed from all parts of the stand. He took the taunts good-naturedly with side-glances at Marjory who seemed amused at the banter. It was easy to assume this form of bravado—exchanging jibes with hostile supporters—for he felt reasonably safe in a crowd. But it was different assuming the same bravado while facing Bimbo, for instance, in what he called his "Torture Chamber." Where was that place, anyway? And how could he find it?

Crack!

"There goes another homer!" screamed a

South High rooter. "Bimbo's second of the day! Look at that ball travel, will you? Wham! She lit on the roof across the street! Yea, Bimbo! ... That makes ten runs for us. Ten to nothing! What a ball game! . . . Who said these Waynesboro boys had a team?"

"Speed Durgan said so!" joshed another rooter, slapping the North High spectator on the back. "He had all he could do to beat 'em! How many hits did they get off you, Speed? And how many runs?"

"Don't rub it in!" teased a third South High supporter. "He feels bad enough as it is! You came over here to see your finish, didn't you? That's what we're going to do to your team—only worse and more of it!"

"We didn't try to beat Waynesboro as badly as we could!" protested Speed, unable to let the taunts go unchallenged. "I just breezed along. What's the use of pitching your head off like your pitcher's been doing?"

"Say—he pitches like that all the time!"

"I hope he keeps on, then—because he'll have his arm burned out by the time he faces us!"

"Razzberries!"

"You mean—carnations!" retorted Speed. "No bird can pitch like Siano's been going to-day and last. It's just not human!"

"Ivan *isn't* human!" declared an ardent rooter. "Did you just discover it? He's a wizard! He can pitch any two other pitchers into the ground! You'll be lucky to go the route with him—especially the way Bimbo's lamming that ball!"

Speed could feel his temper rising.

"Yeah, you fellows have made a noise like this before and you've had an awful time beating us. If it hadn't been for a couple of flukes . . . !"

"You mean—if you hadn't blown up!" cried someone.

Speed half raised in his seat, only to feel Marjory's hand on his arm.

"Don't let them get you all worked up," she said, with a quietness that was calming. "Don't you see that's just what they're trying to do? They're getting a kick out of it!"

Speed looked about him sheepishly. He'd given way to his tendency again—of taking everything too seriously—of being too much concerned about what was said or aimed at him.

"You're right," he said to Marjory. "I've got to watch myself on this. That's one of my troubles . . . !"

A great cheer went up as South High finished the game with Siano's striking out of Waynesboro's last batsman in the first of the ninth. With South High ahead, ten to nothing, it was not necessary for them to take their last bats.

"Great stuff, fellows!" complimented an extremely pleased Bimbo, glancing toward the stands where North High's pitching star had been sitting. "You certainly put on a show today! Some pitching, Ivan! Only three measly hits off you—and no runs! Boy, you're sure in wonderful shape! How's the arm feel?"

"Like another nine innings!" grinned Ivan.

"What do you think of our pitcher now?" persisted the fan who had asked this same question of Speed several innings earlier.

"I think, if he keeps on, he'll amount to something some day," replied Speed, tongue in his cheek.

The South High rooters howled.

"You'd hate to compliment a guy, wouldn't you?"

"How much better pitcher do you think you are?"

"Well, that would be telling," was Speed's answer, as he sought to push his way through the crowd with Marjory. "You birds had better wait and find out!"

"It won't be long now!" sang someone. "Two more weeks and then your team will be visiting our ball park to take a sock on the nose! We're going to make it three straight over you, too! And it won't even be close! We've got the pitcher this year so Bimbo won't have to do it all!"

"They're certainly a cocky bunch on this side of town!" Speed whispered to Marjory. "How do you stand it?"

"I enjoy it for a change!" was Marjory's frank retort. "After coming from a side of town that's so paralyzed by the other side that it apologizes for living!"

"It's not that bad!" protested Speed.

"Almost!" declared Marjory. "I didn't realize how much South has you fellows buffaloed until we moved over here. It's a wonder you don't pay tribute to Bimbo and his gang because they let you breathe!"

"Our time's coming!" predicted Speed. "One of these days we're going to make the South Side crowd look sick!"

"I'd like to see you do it!" said Marjory, "instead of talking about it. If you want to know the truth—I'm beginning to lean in favor of South. You'll have to really show me something to get back in favor!"

"We'll show you plenty inside the next two weeks!" vowed Speed, who smarted under her prodding. "If I could only locate the place they took me to when they smeared on the paint . . . ! What we'd do to that place!"

"I imagine," said Marjory, dryly. "Steer as clear of it as you could!"

The two were now upon the field, walking toward a park exit. As they did so they were hailed by a familiar, uniformed figure who came trotting from the dugout to greet them.

"Hello, Marj! Hello, Speed!" he called.

"Congratulations, Bimbo!" was Marjory's welcome. "You played a great game!"

"Thanks! How'd you like the exhibition, Speed?" South High's captain and home run hitter was grinning broadly.

"First rate!" replied Speed, a bit fussed. "Little one sided, however. No use drubbing them so hard. I didn't let myself out against Waynesboro. They scored some runs but we were always ahead and I could have borne down any time needed."

"Well, you're going to have to bear down with all you've got when you play us!" warned Bimbo. "Because with Ivan pitching shut-out ball, one run's about going to decide the game. And I do like homers!"

"So I see!" observed Speed. "Well, just try to get another against me! You'll be lucky if you get on base!"

"Now, Speed, have a heart!" mocked Bimbo. "Goodbye, old North Sider, and I don't want to see you on this side of town again till you have come over here to play us, understand?"

"He'll come over here any time he wants to!" declared Marjory. "Won't you Speed?"

"Sure I will!" answered Speed, with great assumed defiance.

Speed could feel Bimbo's smirking smile following him as he led Marjory away. How he detested the fellow! He'd never met anyone who could irritate or antagonize him so much over apparently little or nothing! And yet, Marjory had told him that she liked Bimbo! At that he appeared to be a man of his word for Speed wasn't being molested. Beyond the good-natured razzing he had received from the South High crowd, there had been no suggestion of a "rough on rats" treatment. But there was no doubt that Bimbo had meant what he said when he had issued the warning for Speed to make himself a minus quantity on the South Side from now on.

"I'll be seeing you soon," Speed assured Marjory as he left her at her door and turned back toward his car.

"Good for you!" smiled Marjory. "I'm glad you're not letting this Bimbo person bluff you!"

But once Speed had left Marjory his attitude of assurance vanished. He could feel trouble in the air. Things were rapidly coming to a head. There had been considerable sniping by both sides but no big show-down had occurred in some time. As leader of the North Side bunch, if he was to hold their respect, he would have to plan and execute some daring move against Bimbo's cohorts. At present he was in a most unenviable position. A procedure was being forced upon him which he would give most anything to be able to escape from. But as much as he feared the consequences, he feared the loss of respect the more! What his own fellows and what Marjory might think of him did he show the white feather! He could sense that he was actually on trial at the present moment.

"I'll whip this thing!" he resolved, as he drove away. "It's been growing on me like a mushroom. But I'll force myself to snap out of it! I'll give Bimbo and his gang the surprise of their lives!"

Hardly had Speed so declared himself than a car crossed the street intersection ahead of him, loaded with South Side fellows.

"There's Bimbo now!" Speed exclaimed, breathlessly. "I wonder where he's taking the gang? Guess I'll follow!"

Turning after them, Speed kept a block behind, prepared to veer off on a side street should his presence be discovered.

"Uh huh!" he cried, excitedly, as he saw the car come to a stop in an alleyway near an embankment. "Looks like they're going to their hangout! Boy—if they are—what a break of luck for me!"

The South Side fellows piled out of the auto and hurried up the slope toward the rear of a large building which Speed, who had pulled his car to the curb, recognized as the South Oakland Warehouse. Waiting an appreciable moment, Speed crept down the alley on foot until he could get a good view of the back of the building. It was built up on a steel framework in back because the front faced on a street level much higher.

"Sure enough!" observed Speed. "There they go—under the building! Pretty clever hideaway! So that's where they took me! . . . Just about sixty-two steps up the embankment, too, as I counted! Well, well! You guys are going to think that lightning's struck that place in a few days!"

With this a highly elated Speed Durgan quickly retraced his steps, jumped into his father's car, and drove off rapidly in the direction of North Oakland.

CHAPTER VI

REVENGE IS SWEET

FOR the first time in the history of the athletic rivalry between North and South High Schools, both baseball nines completed their schedules undefeated up to their all-important clash. Virtually a state championship was to be decided for the town of Oakland as a consequence.

"It's going to be a battle that Oakland can't lose!" chuckled an impartial fan. "Only North or South can lose but Oakland's bound to win. And just maybe we don't grow baseball players in this town! Man alive! What a game we're going to see!"

Citizens on both sides of the river could talk of little else but the impending conflict. The rivalry expressed by the high schools had somehow become symbolic of the rivalry which merchants and townspeople had felt as a whole. Whichever team, then, might emerge triumphant, would establish supremacy for its side of town—a supremacy which would be flaunted just as enthusiastically by the elders.

And two days before the game, one Speed Durgan, meeting his team members by appointment after dark, nervously outlined a plan.

"Bimbo knows that I'm supposed to call on Marj tonight," he informed his followers. "I've made sure of that. And Bimbo's told Marj not to be surprised if I don't show up. But I've got to show up, at least, or Marj will think I've been scared out. Now here's my scheme . . ."

Seventeen determined youths gathered closer about him, intent on every word. All of them carried flashlights and some were equipped with axes.

"Bimbo's almost certain to try to way-lay me. He's threatened to make it hot for me if I tried to visit Marj again so I expect he'll be waiting near her home again. But he's going to get the shock of his life because I'm taking four of you fellows in the car with me. I want you to crouch down out of sight and, if I'm jumped on, then you pop out and join the free-for-all."

"With these axes?" grinned Salty.

"No, you dumbbell! Those are to be used for wrecking their shack under the warehouse!"
(102)

"I was just thinking," joshed Salty, "how easy it would be for us to cut Bimbo down to our own size with these!"

But Salty's attempt at humor was lost on the moment. Speed was too eager to get his plan in operation. He was driving himself to go through with the idea now. North High had never before gone forth on so bold a venture. Its greatest chance of success depended upon its sheer audacity.

"Chances are that most of Bimbo's bunch will be with him at whatever point he tries to get me!" removed Speed. "So, while we're holding them off, you fellows under Teaser Burke, sneak under the warehouse and get in your dirty work. I don't know just what you'll find under there . . . but clean the whole place out and make a get-away as quickly as possible!"

"But what if you birds are caught?" asked Teaser. "Won't you take an awful drubbing when Bimbo and his gang find out?"

"That's a risk we've got to run!" decided Speed, grimly, refusing to think of the possible consequences. "Salty, Floyd, Steve and Hank— you're to go with me!"

"S-say, I'm better with an axe than I am in a . . . er . . . hand-to-hand battle!" protested Floyd. "Maybe you'd better transfer me . . ."

"You'll be okay when we go into action!" assured Salty. "You're just nervous now like a soldier is before he goes over the top. I can't see you surrendering to Bimbo without a struggle!"

"N-no, you're right, there!" admitted Floyd, feelingly. "This seems like a pretty reckless enterprise to me!"

"It's worth trying," said Speed. "If we can put it over it's bound to have a tremendous affect upon Bimbo's gang. Maybe it'll send 'em so high in the air that they'll forget to ride us during the game! At any rate, it'll feel good to have the shoe on the other foot for awhile. I'm getting tired of everyone saying we're afraid of those bozos! We may be afraid—but we've got nerve enough to hand 'em a taste of their own medicine . . . which ought to give 'em a pretty good idea of the way we're going to sail into 'em on the diamond!"

"Atta boy, Speed!" commended Salty, slapping Speed on the back. "And just when I'd begun to think you didn't have the stuff! Now you've hatched up a plan that's due to get the stuffing knocked out of all of us! But I'm for you just the same! Lead on!"

"Teaser," instructed Speed, "you get off with your bunch first. Do some scouting around the back of that warehouse before you go under it . . . to be sure the gang isn't there. Meanwhile we'll be doing our best to act as decoys and draw Bimbo's fire as long as we can. Then let's meet back here at the ball grounds and swap reports!"

"Very good!" responded Teaser, thumbing at the fellows who were to go with him. "Here's where we torture Bimbo's Torture Chamber!"

"And here's where I go through the worst torture of all!" Speed told himself, as he led the way to his car. "I'm trembling like a leaf. Hope none of the guys notice it!"

On a hunch that Bimbo might lay somewhat the same plans to capture him which he had employed before, Speed stopped his car opposite the alleyway that ran behind Marjory Coulter's home.

"Salty, you can drive a car, can't you?"

"You know it!"

"All right, then! There's just a chance that Bimbo's got his car in the alley again. You sneak down there and, if he has, you drive it around the corner. Then, if they pounce on me and carry me back to where his car was, they won't be able to get away and the rest of you fellows can come to my rescue."

"I can drive a car, too!" volunteered Floyd, uneasily. "Why don't you let me do that?"

"No, Floyd!" grinned Salty. "We need you to do the fighting! You stick with Speed!"

"Good grief!" moaned the nervous North Sider.

Drawing up in front of Marjory's house, a tingling Speed caught a glimpse of her face at the window. He waved. So far, so good. It was so dark that he could not see whether anyone was lurking behind the hedge in the shadows. At this last instant he found himself wishing that there wouldn't be . . . that Bimbo's threat had all been a bluff. But an uncanny something told him that he was going to meet with a similar unpleasant experience . . . a sudden lunging attack. And yet, with the knowledge that three of his buddies were tensely awaiting just such an attack, ready to spring out and rush to his defense—Speed felt a surge of courage. He placed his hand on the gate and swung it open. Marjory's figure appeared in the doorway. With eyes upon her, he suddenly saw her stop and place a hand to her lips as though horrified. Then, from a tree whose branches overhung the sidewalk, Speed heard a scraping sound. He started to step aside as the avalanche hit him, bearing him to earth. In the next moment all was pandemonium. There were shouts and grunts as a swarm of attackers from hedge and tree, tried to subdue a desperately fighting Speed; then—surprised cries as Floyd, Steve and Hank threw themselves into the melee— all this punctuated by a scream from Marjory and the stern voice of Mr. Coulter who had rushed out on the porch, shouting: "Boys! Boys!"

Despite all he could do, Speed once more felt the gunny sack pulled tight over his head and himself being hustled along toward the Coulter's back yard.

"We'll settle this in the alley!" said a voice which Speed recognized at Bimbo's. "So you fellows want to rouse the neighborhood, do you?"

"You guys did the hollering!" accused Floyd, leaping on Bimbo's back and being immediately tossed off, only to pick himself up and come rushing back for more. "You've told us what to do long enough! Now we're going to tell you . . . !"

"Get out of Coulter's yard before he raises a fuss!" were Bimbo's instructions to his gang. "We'll capture the whole bunch and . . . !"

"Yes you will!" panted Steve Clawson, who was Speed's battery mate and the sturdiest man on the team. "Let's gang on Bimbo, fellows! Put him out of the way, then the rest will be easy!"

Out-numbered more than two to one, the four North Siders were putting up a frenzied resistance, aided by their opponents' enforced retreat from the Coulter yard. On reaching the alleyway, however, there was every indication that the tide would turn.

"Hello!" bellowed an enraged Bimbo, looking about. "Where's my car?"

"Your *car*?" shouted his gang members, astounded.

"Some more of their monkey business!" accused Bimbo, turning to Speed who was struggling to remove the gunny sack. "What we'll do to them!"

The attack was renewed with greater fury. Floyd and Steve made for Bimbo at the same time and Bimbo's henchmen leaped in to tear them off. Speed, meanwhile, managed to jerk the gunny sack off. Finding himself in the midst of flailing arms and kicking legs, he saw an opportunity to slip the bag over the head of a besieged Bimbo. He did it so quickly that no one noticed it in the excitement. The alley was dark and Bimbo, with the noose of the gunny sack drawn tight, became the target for his own men who mistook him for their leading adversary. Amazed at what they took to be Speed's great show of fighting strength, four of Bimbo's followers bore their own chieftain to the ground and gave him a sound thumping.

"Let up! Let up!" begged Bimbo in a muffled voice.

"Speed!" yelled Steve, thinking he was the form on the ground. "Fight 'em! That's it! Give it to 'em! We'll be with you in a minute!"

Speed, rushing up, grabbed Steve's arm.

"That's Bimbo—you boob!" he said in Steve's ear. "Get Floyd and Hank out of this and let's beat it while the beating's good."

Jerking free of their assailants, the four North Siders who had given a valiant account of themselves, rushed down the alley, leaving an exasperated Bimbo, sputtering and fuming as he tried to remove the gunny sack, with the cord knotted about his neck.

"There's Salty with Bimbo's car!" pointed out Speed, as he and his followers reached the corner. "Floyd, you and Hank go with him. Tell him to hit for our side of town. Steve, you come with me! I'm going to pick up my car!"

The four acted with great dispatch. Salty was off almost before Floyd and Hank could scramble inside. Steve and Speed had to run for it. Marjory and her father had just returned to the porch after having followed out to the backyard.

"Speed!" she called, as he jumped in his car.

"Sorry!" Speed answered. "I can't stop now! I'll get in touch with you later!"

"These boys!" stormed Mr. Coulter, as he

watched the car, with Speed at the wheel, swerve around the corner out of sight. "They're holy terrors!"

"They're wonderful!" exclaimed Marjory, impulsively. "I . . . er . . . mean—the North Siders! Oh, Dad—maybe North Oakland will win this year—after all!"

"Bah!" said Mr. Coulter, as he went into the house. "You girls are as hopeless as the boys!"

Half an hour later, highly excited and jubilant auto parties commenced arriving at the North Side ball grounds. The group led by Teaser Burke proudly displayed a panel bearing the skull and cross bones, painted in red.

"Chief Bimbo's insignia!" said Teaser. "And here's the big bone he used for his gavel to call the meetings to order! We've all of us got some nice little souvenirs of our wrecking party! . . . Say they had it fixed up swell under there! Built the shack out of loose boards and sides of drygoods boxes. We tore it all down and took it outside and built a bonfire in the alley. Nothing left now but the ashes. Anything of real value we left in a pile under the building, such as books and clothing. But there won't be any more torturing done in that Chamber for a while—believe you me!"

Speed's arrival brought cheers and a great shout of laughter went up with Salty's exhibition of Bimbo's automobile.

"What a field day we had!" roared Steve.

"You mean—field *night!*" corrected Teaser. "Bimbo's forces have been put to complete rout. Speed, you out-Napoleoned Napoleon! The king is dead—long live the king! What a body-blow for Bimbo! He'll never recover! Whoopie! Bring on your South High baseball team! We'll eat it alive!"

Jubilation reigned—it was so seldom the North Side had anything on the South Side to crow about.

"Let's let the air out of Bimbo's automobile tires!" someone suggested. "Then you call him up, Speed, and tell him where he can find his machine."

"That's an idea!" cried another.

And the tires were deflated as the car stood in the field.

"We really ought to drain the gas off, too!" suggested Salty. "Make it really hard for him to get his car home!"

"No, we've made it tough enough now," decided Speed. "We don't want to destroy anything of actual value. Thing for us to do is to go home and to bed. We'll probably hear plenty about this in the morning. And we want to watch our step! It won't be exactly healthy to be seen in South Oakland before game time. If I don't miss my guess, they're dying to get their hands on us this minute!"

"We should worry!" laughed Teaser. "Boy, this makes up for a lot of hard raps I've taken from those South Side babies! Do I feel good?"

The happy crowd, with morale restored, dispersed. Speed, in the company of Steve and a disheveled Floyd, made for the nearest drug store where Speed entered a phone booth. While he was getting the number, Floyd approached a drug clerk.

"What you got that's good for cuts and bruises?"

"A number of things!" smiled the clerk.

"All right," said Floyd, "give 'em to me! There's not a spot on my body that something hasn't happened to!"

"Been in a fight?"

"Have I? I've licked the whole South Side!"

After two busy signals and a wrong number, Speed finally got his party.

"Hello, this Bimbo? . . . Suppose you'd like to know where your car is? . . . I thought so . . . Now, don't get so hot about it or we won't tell you! . . . Your car is parked in the middle of our baseball diamond! . . . What's that? . . . We *will* not! You come and get it! . . . When will you call for it? . . . No, sir! If the car's not gone by morning it'll be given away or sold for junk. Come over with a gang, if you like. We won't touch you so long as the only thing you touch is your car. But look out otherwise!"

Speed felt better as he hung up the receiver on a fellow who had been giving him orders for several years. And it was only after he had gotten himself home and safely to bed that the reaction set in and the let-down came of the strain he had been under. Then he fell into a fit of laughing which almost amounted to a state of hysteria.

"Bimbo, the Great has fallen!" he kept repeating, this declaration sounding funnier each time he repeated it. "Bimbo, the Great! Oh, ha, ha, ha! Ho, ho, ho! I wonder what Marjory thinks now! I can just see Bimbo trying to get those tires pumped up and his car off our ball field. Well, here's one time when we certainly put one over! Now, if we can top this by winning the game . . . !"

Speed Durgan, North High's pitching ace, slept soundly.

CHAPTER VII

TO THE VICTORS

SUCH excitement had not been seen on both sides of the river in years as that which prevailed in the town of Oakland on the day of the baseball clash between North and South High Schools. News of the last escapade in the series of retributive disturbances had spread through the city causing many exclamations of surprise at the unexpected daring of the North Siders.

"Maybe the worm's commenced to turn at last!" said a North Oakland merchant, hopefully. "We'll know today! And I'm going to close my store for the game to give the boys all encouragement possible!"

A revived spirit was apparent throughout the North Side whose colors had formerly seemed to droop in meek surrender to the dominating South Side. Across the river, citizens were already crying for a new revenge. Bimbo and his gang must get even for this audacious raid of the North Siders which had succeeded in so completely outwitting them and reducing their very stronghold to ashes. Not in the history of the great Oakland feud, had such a devastating attack been perpetrated.

"And we thought all along that Speed lacked nerve!" demoaned Kinky. "He just tricked us into believing he didn't have—and then pulled this on us!"

"I still don't think he's got nerve!" declared Bimbo, grudgingly. "We just got him in a jam and he had to get out the best he could. The breaks happened to be with him or we'd have made him look sick!"

"But how about our shack?" asked Lieutenant Sam Wade, sadly. "What happened to that wasn't any accident!"

"N-no, I admit that!" said Bimbo, reluctantly. "Say—I wonder how he got next to where our hangout was? Do you suppose Marjory told him?"

"How would she know about it?"

"Why, I . . . er . . . I may have mentioned it to her," stammered Bimbo, face flushing.

"Well, of all the ivory-topped boneheads!"

cried Sam, impulsively. "A . . . er . . . excuse me, Chief!"

Bimbo glowered. "I'm going to see her and check up on this! If she's been double-crossing us . . . !"

"What can you do about it?" demanded Stub Hanley. "If you spilled the beans . . . ? You didn't give her the information in secret, did you?"

"Why, I . . . I believe I did!" said Bimbo, trying to recall. "I told her nobody knew where our hide-away was, but us!"

"You ought to have known better than tell anything to a girl!" reproved Al Cort. "They can't keep secrets!"

"Yes they can!" declared Ivan Siano, stoutly. "My sister's known where our hangout was for some time and she hasn't given us away— not even to mother and dad."

"How'd she find out?"

"She saw us go in the alley one day and she watched."

"We got too careless, that's what's the matter!" decided Sam. "We figured nobody would get wise. We should have posted a lookout there."

"It's too late now," said Kinky. "Now that the warehouse people know we had a shack under their building, it's all off!"

"I'm going to have a talk with Marj!" decided Bimbo. "I'll bet she's the key to this whole thing. I've been a boob all right for saying anything to her. She probably was the brains behind the job just like she was on the Costume Ball affair! Oh, boy—have I been simple? Hit me on the head, Sam—I deserve it!"

But Bimbo's followers were lenient with him in his moment of despondency and confessed weakness. They knew that Bimbo had great come-back powers; that he bounded back against his opponents like an irrepressible rubber ball; the harder he was hit, the higher he bounded. The chances were that Bimbo's answer to this humiliating defeat of his forces would be an outstandingly brilliant performance on the diamond. He would be toeing the plate every time at bat obsessed with a savage desire to drive every ball pitched by Speed Durgan out of the park.

"It's going to be just too bad for North High now!" Kinky whispered significantly to Sam

Wade, and Bimbo's first lieutenant nodded in agreement.

"Bimbo's on the warpath now as he never was before!" Sam rejoined, in a low voice. "North probably figures they've got our goats for a change but they don't know Bimbo if they think that. He's never really been crossed until he took this on the chin. That baby just thrives on opposition. The best thing North could have done was to have laid low because Bimbo'll not be satisfied till he's made them eat their own dust!"

All of which promised plenty of action and which accounted for the capacity crowd that packed South High's ball park, impatiently clamoring for the game to begin!

Boos and hisses greeted the appearance of North High's team on the field. These were quickly erased by a cheer from the North High supporters who had invaded the South Side a thousand strong.

"South Oakland and North Oakland just love to hate each other!" laughed a spectator. "It makes life so much more interesting!"

"It's going to be a battle of pitchers today!"

said another, looking the rival hurlers over as they warmed up. "Ivan and Speed seem to be in top form. Hello—see Speed make that wild pitch?"

The ball topped catcher Steve Clawson's head by several feet and the crowd roared. Steve went back after the ball, recovered it, and—instead of throwing it to his pitcher—walked back for a conference.

"Getting ready to throw the game away again?" called Bimbo from the dugout.

Speed acknowledged the taunt with a mocking bow and grin. But, to a discerning Steve, North High's pitching ace appeared anything but self-possessed.

"Steady down, Speed. You're warming up too fast. What's the matter? Nervous?"

Speed drew a deep breath. "I—I'm always a little nervous before a game," he said. "You know that. Nothing to worry about."

"You're thinking too much," cautioned Steve. "Don't hold yourself so tense. This is just another ball game—that's the attitude to take."

"It's the last ball game I'll pitch for the school . . . the last you'll catch," reminded Speed. "We've got to make good!"

"Sure we'll make good . . . but take it easy! Let's see the old stuff in there now . . . and not too fast!"

Steve paced off the approximate distance between pitcher's box and home plate, turned about and held out his glove as a target.

"All right, big boy! Smack it in the groove! Put over that last strike!"

Bimbo, emerging from the dugout, strolled over, hands on hips, to a point where he could study the opposing pitcher. It was ten minutes to game time. Bimbo's action caused all attention to be centered for the moment upon Speed. Apparently flustered, Speed's next pitch was low, so low that it struck the ground in front of catcher Steve Clawson who scooped the ball in on the bound.

"Not so good!" remarked Bimbo.

Speed's face reddened, and South High rooters shouted their glee. If North's star hurler was this wild before the game, what would he be like at the start? The next pitch was high and wide, and Steve Clawson wisely called to Speed that this was "enough." He could tell that his pitcher was getting more unnerved every pitch.

Bimbo turned and sauntered over to the box close to the playing field where a certain girl was sitting. His movement was deliberate and in plain view of Speed who had gone into North High's dugout across the diamond.

"Well, Marj!" Bimbo drawled. "Looks like I'd be taking you to South High's party to-night!"

Marjory smiled, pretending not to have gotten the inference. "What makes you think so?"

"The way your friend was warming up," Bimbo replied. "Remember what I told you about him. You watch and see!"

"You can't tell me anything about him after what happened night before last!" Marjory rejoined, sharply.

"Yeah, that's what I want to ask you about!" said Bimbo, a bit sheepishly. "Did you tip Speed off to where our shack was?"

Marjory looked at Bimbo a moment, color rising in her cheeks.

"I most certainly did not!"

"Well . . . er . . . did you help him scheme against us?"

"I had nothing to do with it, Carl Bailey!"

"All right! I believe you! Only I can't figure out how that guy, Speed, ever did what he did—alone!"

"You're still not willing to give him credit, are you?" derided Marjory. "But you're going to have to, after today!"

Bimbo, grinning broadly, doffed his cap. "What time shall I call for you this evening?" he asked.

Marjory made an impish face at him for answer.

Catcher Steve Clawson, on reaching the dugout, reported at once to Coach Hart.

"Speed's stuff is not working," he announced.

"I thought not," said the Coach, concernedly. "What do you think's the trouble?"

"Same old complex," replied Steve. "He's a whiz against any outfit but this. Can't get Bimbo off his mind. All Bimbo had to do was look him over and Speed went to pieces. I thought he was going to be hot today, too!"

Coach Hart considered. "Of course I could start Jed Russell but I'd rather chance it with Speed, regardless. It's ridiculous for Speed to feel this way—he's easily the best pitcher in the state. Defeated only twice in almost three seasons . . ."

"But by the *same* team!" emphasized Steve. "And that's what's on his mind now. He'd give anything to beat this jinx but the more he thinks about it, the more it gets him!"

"It's not the team he fears, it's Bimbo!" declared the coach. "If there was only some way . . ."

"I have it!" cried Steve. "He's only afraid of Bimbo at the bat. If you could instruct him to walk Bimbo every time up. . . ?"

"I'll do it!" decided Coach Hart. "Oh, Speed—here a minute, will you?"

A serious-faced youth arose from the bench and came over.

"Yes, Coach?"

"Steve and I have been talking. We've been figuring out a way to break the backbone of South's batting attack. Naturally, the man we want to stop most of all is their heaviest hitter, Bimbo. And the only way to be sure of stopping him is to pass him!"

Speed stared. "But is that very sporting?"

"It's baseball," said Coach Hart. "It may not

particularly please South High rooters . . . and you may be accused of being afraid to pitch to Bimbo. What of it? There's many a good pitcher who might better have paid Bimbo that tribute than to have seen the game disappear over the fence. Not that you might be unable to retire him safely enough—but when Bimbo connects solidly with the ball, it usually travels far and something tells me that we're going to need to hold the score down! This Ivan Siano looks good to me!"

"He *is* good," conceded Speed. "I like your idea, Coach, the more I think it over. It'll probably make Bimbo hopping mad but it's a sure way of disposing of him with as little damage as possible!"

"Exactly!" seconded Coach Hart. "So you just go out there on the mound and pitch your usual game, resting easy in your mind about Bimbo . . . because this method will take care of him nicely."

Speed looked his relief. "That *does* take a load off my mind," he admitted.

Highly partisan as was the crowd, South High supporters abandoned their razzing tactics to give their opponents from across the river a sportsmanlike cheer as North High came to bat for the first half of the opening inning.

Teaser Burke, in apparent appreciation of this cheer, immediately hit the first ball pitched by Ivan, the so-called "Terrible", for three bases.

"Whoa!" yelled South High rooters, dazed at the suddenness of the blow. "That's far enough! Eyes open out there, Ivan!"

Teaser's smashing triple had caused great jubilation in the North High dugout. Coach Hart, realizing the psychological advantage which his team possessed if it was capable of following up, ordered Floyd Tenney, next at bat, to hit at the first ball pitched.

Smack!

"Yea!" shrieked North Side fans. "A run's in! Atta boy, Floyd! Nice little line single over second! Couldn't be better! What's all this noise we've been hearing over Ivan, the Terrible? He's terrible all right! Better take him out!"

Kinky Roxburg, South High's catcher, came out from behind the plate to talk things over.

"You think they've got our signals?" Ivan asked, anxiously. "Hitting that first ball stuff . . . right at the start, too!"

"Naw!" scoffed Kinky, though he was actually worried. "That was just accidental. Waste the next one, though. Maybe we'll nip the runner going down to second."

Ivan returned to the mound, taking his time on the next throw. One run in and only two balls pitched was enough to upset any pitcher.

"Settle down in there!" Bimbo called from his position in centerfield.

Ivan raised his arms over his head. The pitch was purposely wide but the batter swung on it and missed. As catcher Kinky Roxburg had divined, North High's runner on first, had darted for second on the pitch—attempting the hit and run.

"Safe!" shouted the umpire as Floyd slid in and Kinky's peg to the base was high.

"Man on second and nobody out!" cried a North High fan. "Good chance for another score!"

A slashing drive followed which was knocked down by the second baseman on a remarkable stop. Floyd raced to third but the baseman made a great throw to first to nip the batsman, receiving a fine hand for his effort.

"That's the old support!" pitcher Ivan was heard to tell his infield.

But Salty Peters was now at bat—hitting number four or clean-up position for North High. Strangely enough he occupied the same position in the batting order and the same position in the field that the renowned Bimbo did for his team . . . but here the similarity ended. While Salty was a good hitter, with an especial ability for producing in a pinch, he made no claims of being in Bimbo's murderous clouting class.

"I'll be satisfied if I can just meet the ball when it's needed," Salty had said.

And, while he was not entirely satisfied with the long high fly which flew off his bat to be gobbled in by Bimbo out near the fence, the drive did serve the purpose of scoring Floyd from third with North's second run of the inning!

"Nothing to it!" taunted a North Sider. "You fellows give up while the score's still respectable—or do you want to take an awful beating?"

"Wait till we get our bats!" challenged North High fans. "Your pitcher won't look so hot, either!"

And Ivan Siano's admirers found cause to cheer with his striking out of the next batter which retired the side with North leading, two runs to nothing.

"A nice two run lead for you to work on!" said Coach Hart to Speed as he left for the mound.

"It's a lead I'm going to hold!" Speed said, grimly.

He felt differently about the game now. His team-mates had gotten to the opposing pitcher at the start and Bimbo was to be treated with kid gloves. These two factors should go a long way toward deciding the game.

"There's nothing to worry about," Speed told himself. "All I've got to do is pitch ball!"

But, as if the law of compensation was trying to balance baseball matters up, Speed lost South's lead-off hitter after getting two strikes on him when he hit to Floyd Tenney at short, who fumbled.

"That's all right, Floyd," Speed reassured.

"It's *not* all right," ranted Floyd, displeased with himself. "That was an easy chance. I should have had it!"

"Well, get the next one!"

Catcher Steve Clawson won a burst of applause when the next batter, trying to bunt, hit a pop foul which Steve grabbed after a run. One down and a man on first.

"We're all with you today!" Teaser shouted to Speed.

North High's pitcher nodded. Sam Wade, one of Bimbo's leading henchman was at the plate, waving his bat menacingly, and waiting in the batter's box was Bimbo himself, fingering his black bat and looking toward the fence.

"Get those two runs back!" the South Oakland crowd was demanding.

Speed pitched and Sam Wade hit—a sizzling drive down to short. But Floyd, eager to atone for his error, made a frenzied dive and came up with the ball. He tossed to second for a force-out of the runner but second baseman Hank Perry missed doubling the batter at first by an eyelash.

"Good boy, Floyd!" cried Speed, greatly relieved. "You pulled me out of a hole that time!"

"I couldn't let you down again!" was Floyd's retort. "Come on, Speed—the old zip. We'll take number three!"

Two down and the maddest sort of cheers . . . everyone in the South High stands on their feet in a customary form of greeting to their favorite home run hitter. Bimbo took the ovation quietly enough. He was the acme of confidence as he strode to the plate, polishing his black bat against his trouser legs. A home run was exactly what was needed to tie the score and he had no intentions of letting the ball remain in the park if he but connected.

"Stick it in there!" he growled at Speed, swishing his bat across the plate. "You know you can't pitch it past me! Might as well give me my annual home run now because I'm going to . . ."

"Ball one!" announced the umps.

Bimbo looked back at North's catcher and then out at the pitcher. It couldn't be that they were going to pass him? Naturally, Speed wouldn't give him a good ball to hit at if he could help it. But something seemed fishy about this! Bimbo, scowling, crowded the plate that he might reach across and swing at a wide pitch.

"Look out!"

The ball, leaving the temporarily unsteady hand of pitcher Speed Durgan, whizzed down the pitching lane, not high and outside as catcher Steve Clawson had ordered, but high and *inside!* And Bimbo, who was already crowding the plate, taken entirely unaware, was not able to duck in time. The horsehide struck him over the right ear, making a sharp crack as it did so, and felling him in his tracks.

"Oh, I—I'm sorry!" gasped Speed, a sick feeling in his stomach as he saw South's star hitter go down.

Steve, nearest to him, helped his adversary up, Bimbo recovering quickly enough to make a rush at Speed who came hurrying from the mound to see about the possible injury.

"You did that on purpose!" Bimbo accused, swinging a fist which narrowly missed connecting with the point of Speed's chin.

Steve grabbed the enraged Bimbo and pulled him back, aided by the umpire.

"Take your base!" ordered the arbiter.

"But I . . . this guy's had it in for me! He deliberately pitched a bean ball!" protested Bimbo, hand to his head. "Of all the dirty . . . !"

"It was a wild pitch!" declared Steve. "I called for another pitch-out and he lost control. Go take your base!"

"I never purposely dusted off a batter in my life!" Speed denied, hotly.

"I'll get you for this!" Bimbo rejoined, shaking his fist.

The stands were in an uproar over the incident, sentiment about evenly divided. Bimbo, quick to play on this sentiment, trotted down to first, still ejaculating and urging his team-mates to take a hand in driving Speed out of the box.

"Never mind that bag of hot air!" called Steve. "Pitch to me, Speed, old boy!"

With heart in his mouth, Speed toed the pitcher's slab. He could feel the palpitation in his temples. The happening had upset him. It wasn't pleasant to have South High supporters howling at him, calling him a "bean ball artist"; a "dirty player"; and, a "poor sport". He knew,

(102)

himself, that his hitting of Bimbo had been unintentional but how could he prove it to this highly excited mob of South Siders?

Speed's first two pitches to the next batter were so wide of the plate that catcher Steve Clawson barely managed to catch them.

"Don't walk him!" begged the infield. "Let him hit, Speed! We'll get him for you!"

"Speed's done for!" shouted Bimbo, leading off from first. "And he ought to be done for! Any guy who'd . . . !"

"Strike one!" bellowed the umps.

Speed's pitch had skimmed over the outside corner of the plate. He was desperately trying to hang on, to get ahold of himself. Bimbo wasn't going to drive him out of the game on something that was purely accidental . . . no matter what Bimbo thought of it . . . or tried to make his crowd think!

"Strike two!" The batter had let the second pitch go by in the hopes it would be a ball. Now the count was two and two.

"That's pitching!" commended Steve, breathing easier. "They can't touch you when you breeze 'em in that way!"

Forced to swing at the next pitch or be counted out, the batter hit a high fly to center which Salty Peters camped under and clutched firmly to retire the side with no runs, pulling Speed out of a bad hole.

"The worst is over," said Steve, putting a hand on Speed's shoulder as the two walked in to the dugout together. "You weathered a tough spot, old man, and you sure showed your stuff under fire. Bimbo tried his best to get your goat, he had all the breaks with him, and yet he couldn't do it! Now that you've steadied down you'll have this bunch eating from your hand, while we'll be getting to this bird, Ivan Siano, for some more runs!"

Steve's prognostication was correct insofar as Speed's pitching was concerned but he missed a guess with reference to South High's slabsman. Ivan, the Terrible, surprised by coming back with a fine brand of hurling and a series of scoreless innings commenced to string along with the two runs put across by North High in the first looming larger and larger.

Speed's encounters with Bimbo at the bat were in the third and the sixth. In the third,

South had one man on base when Bimbo came up and Speed promptly passed him. The fans, believing Speed to still be unnerved at having beaned Bimbo, could not decide whether the base on balls had been intentional. In the sixth, however, when Speed again passed Bimbo with a man on base, the South Side rooters sent up a great hue and cry.

"He's afraid of him!"

"What kind of baseball do you call that?"

"That's good baseball!" rejoined North High fans who thoroughly approved of Speed's procedure, remembering Bimbo's murderous hitting of other years. "Speed knows what he's doing!"

Going into the last of the eighth, North High still led, two to nothing, both pitchers hurling invincible ball. There was every indication that the game would end with the present score and that Speed Durgan had at last succeeded in breaking the spell which had been held over him by his old rivals.

"Going to the party tonight?" Bimbo called out to him from the coaching line. "Who you going with? Marjory's staying on this side of town!"

Speed gave no sign that he heard the taunt. He had scarcely thought of Marjory during the battle. That's right—she had made a bet with Bimbo! And it looked now as though she had won . . . and that he had won, too—the right to take her to North High's annual party! This would be another bitter dose for Bimbo to swallow but he had these doses coming.

Crack! The first batter up had singled sharply to left. It was the first hit that South had made in four innings. From the noise that South High supporters made over it, one would have thought it was the first hit made during the game.

"What did I tell you about that party?" Bimbo shouted.

With a double play in sight on the next hit ball, a roller down to second, Hank Perry gummed up the play and both runners were safe. Two men on and no one down. Speed had not been in such a hole since the opening inning. But he wasn't particularly disturbed about it. He'd been in holes before—and this was just another ball game . . . just another ball game!

"You're going to lose Marjory in just a minute!" razzed Bimbo. "Better make your plans to attend that party alone!"

Speed, for the first time, glanced irritatedly toward the coaching line.

"What's that Bimbo talking about?" a spectator asked.

"Search me!" grinned a South High rooter, "But it probably means something to Speed Durgan!"

Bracing desperately and pitching slowly, determined to retain his shut-out lead, Speed struck out the next batter. But the next dropped a surprise bunt in front of the plate and beat it out while his mates dashed safely to second and third.

"Bases full and only one out!" shrieked South High. "Goodby, ball game!"

"All right, Marjory! I'll be over to see you in just a minute!" yelled Bimbo, looking in the direction of the box where a red-cheeked girl was sitting. "Hey—somebody! Come out here and relieve me on the coaching line. I'm going to be to bat pretty soon!"

"Don't let Bimbo get to bat this inning!" beseeched North High rooters, suddenly panic-stricken.

Steve came out in front of the plate to talk it over.

"How's your arm?"

"Good as ever," assured Speed, conscious that Steve was studying him closely. "We'll pull out of this!"

"We've got to!" said Steve, smacking his fist in his catcher's mitt. "Watch me, now, and don't mind what these nuts holler at you!"

Speed nodded. Inwardly he couldn't help but wonder what Marjory must be thinking at the present moment. She had bet on him; she was expecting him to make good; he had to come through, somehow—he had to! A fly to the outfield meant a run; any kind of a hit meant two runs and a tie score! The situation called for a supreme piece of pitching.

Nervous perspiration stood out upon Speed's forehead as he worked the count up to three balls and two strikes on the next batter with the crowd yelling like mad. He mustn't lose him. A walk meant a run. He mustn't lose him . . . mustn't lose him! . . . . But—he DID! . . . A high fly to right . . . the catch . . . and a run scampering in from third. Runners now left on first and second . . . two out . . . ! Oh, well—North was still in front, two to one. That was a good score—two to one. He shouldn't kick at that. He'd get the next batter for the third out and choke South's last big rally. They'd never get to him in the last of the ninth . . . he'd mow them down, one, two, three!

"Pitch to me, big boy! Pitch to me!" Steve's steady voice from behind the plate. Good old Steve!

"Save me a bat, Al!" called a familiar voice. Bimbo—swinging his ugly black club and stamping about with furious impatience, eager for the kill. HE—was next up! Speed looked at him for an instant and the perspiration seemed to freeze on his forehead. But, no! Bimbo would never get up in this inning because the batter at the plate was going to make the third out! Bimbo wasn't going to take Marjory to the party after all! Marjory was going across the river to a party—across the river . . . where North High would be celebrating the greatest victory of all! . . . Good old Coach Hart! He'd worked out the right system . . . not to let Bimbo get a swipe at the ball! Pass him every time up! . . . Every time up!

"Ball two!" The umpire's voice coming from

what seemed to be a distance—and jarring him.

Ball two? He hardly remembered having pitched the first one but he must have if the umps said "ball two". What was that? . . .Yes, it was ball two all right.

"Don't lose him!" the whole infield was shouting at him.

"Going to the party?" Bimbo seemed to be saying. He was grinning.

"Ball three!"

"No, no! That cut the corner!"

But the umps was shaking his head. You couldn't argue with an umpire. His word was law. But this batter mustn't walk! If he did walk it would fill the bases again and put Bimbo at the bat! Why couldn't he get the ball over the plate? He was walking the wrong man. Bimbo was the fellow he was supposed to walk! . . . But he couldn't walk Bimbo if this man walked because it would force in a run—the tieing run! Everything seemed hazy.

"Strike one!"

"Sure that's a strike!" Speed heard himself mumbling. "And there's another—right in the same place!"

"Ball four!" from the umps, with a jab of the thumb toward first base.

A wild roar from the crowd!

"No, no! That ball was good!" The protest died on Speed's lips.

Bases full and the mighty Bimbo at the bat. He had to face the situation at last! There was no dodging it this time!

"Strike him out!" begged a forlorn voice.

Speed started. The voice had sounded strangely like Marjory's! She was pulling for him to come through. He couldn't fail this time. He'd failed twice before. What was that old saying 'three times and out'? . . .

"You'd better stay for *our* party!" invited Bimbo.

He had entered the batter's box, ominous black bat on his shoulder. Speed gave an anxious glance at the outfield. All three fielders were moving back toward the fence and the park was an insane jumble of noise.

"History about to repeat itself!" shrilled someone.

"History about to be made!" corrected Speed, nervously. "What's that guy mean . . . ?"

"Everything you've got now, Speed! Steam 'em in here! This baby isn't so much. He's over-rated! That's what he is—over-rated!" encouraged Steve.

The infield was talking it up now, trying to drown out all the other things that were being shouted at him. He could even hear Salty's voice drifting in from centerfield.

"Stick with 'em, Speed!"

Well, he'd have to start pitching to this Bimbo. He'd been stalling for time to get his nerves under better control.

"Look out!"

Another pitch dangerously close to Bimbo's head!

"Booh! . . . Booh!" from the stands.

"Trying to scare me, eh?" from Bimbo, who had stepped back in the box. "Well, I don't scare that easy!"

A miserable feeling swept over Speed. Again he hadn't meant to throw the ball near Bimbo. He had simply lost his grip on it and the crowd was giving him credit for . . . !

On the next pitch, Bimbo swung, turning completely around in the batter's box, missing the ball by half a foot. North High fans roared in glee.

"Some hitter, you are!" they jeered. "What's so tough about him, Speed? Strike him out!"

Lips in a tight line, putting everything he had on the ball, Speed pitched again. Once more Bimbo swung viciously and once more he connected with nothing but ozone.

"Yea!" screamed North High supporters, going mad. "You've got *Bimbo's* goat now! He can't even see 'em!"

South High's heavy hitter stepped from the batter's box, scowling deeply. He tapped the dirt from his cleats with his bat and nodded, reassuringly, to his team-mates who besought him from every base.

"Drive us in, Bimbo! Break up this old ball game!"

"One more strike!" begged North High fans. "Give him the gate, Speed! Turn your old fast ball on him!"

"Ball two!" from the umps, and groans from the North High bleachers. The pitch had been a teaser, barely on the outside, which Bimbo had almost been tempted to swing at.

"Two and two!" said someone, nervously. The strain was growing unbearable.

"Everything first!" reminded catcher Steve Clawson. "Remember, two down!"

"He won't even hit it!" predicted a Speed Durgan admirer.

"I won't, eh?" was Bimbo's retort. "I'm going to the party with Marjory on this next pitch!"

Speed, his arms up over his head, ready for the pitch, felt a tremor go through him. Wouldn't that fellow ever shut up about that party? Why talk about it at a time like this? Marjory watching, and . . . !

Socko! The resounding crash of a bat against the ball and a bounding white object between right and center fields. Flashing legs on the bases. One run in . . . two runs . . . three runs . . . and a chest-heaving figure encamped on third, hugging the bag and yelling something about "Marjory! . . . Marjory!"

"That hit just about does it!" someone was saying in a high-pitched voice above the din. "Bimbo's only chance to hit today and did he come through? Oh, mamma! He cleaned the bases!"

A weary and disconsolate Speed Durgan looked out at the scoreboard.

SOUTH HIGH 4
NORTH HIGH 2

And it mattered little to him that the next batter was retired, short to first, for the damage had already been done. There was one faint, glimmering hope. North High had one more time at bat—the first of the ninth. But this hope went the way of most forlorn hopes with Ivan Siano—Ivan, the Terrible, if you please—bearing down so heavily that two North High batsmen went out on strikes and the third fouled out to catcher to send the game into history . . . a history that had, after all, pretty closely repeated itself . . . giving to South High the distinction of having defeated the otherwise invincible Speed Durgan for three consecutive years . . . administering the only defeats that had been scored against him. Some achievement, this!

Crossing the diamond from the dugout, head bowed, unmindful of the tumult about him, Speed felt his arm grasped, and looked up into the face of the grinning Bimbo.

"You were plenty tough today!" he greeted, "Makes me almost sorry I won my bet!"

"Go ahead! Enjoy yourself!" rejoined Speed. "You won fair and square. I . . ."

"Say, listen!" said Bimbo, shouting in his ear to make himself heard above the din. "They tell me you're going to college?"

"Why, I . . . yes . . . I expect to," Speed answered, somewhat taken aback. Why should Bimbo be mentioning college at a time like this?

"Where to?" asked Bimbo.

"Billiter!" Speed replied, his wonderment growing.

At this, Bimbo's grin widened. "That's fine!" he declared, moving off. "Then we'll meet again. I'm going to Winston!"

Speed stopped short and stared after the departing Bimbo, a deeper shade of dejection crossing his face. Winston and Billiter were as bitter rivals in their way as North and South Highs. And here he had looked forward to going to college because he had secretly told himself that it would mean getting away from his old jinx!

For a moment the world seemed a very black place to one Speed Durgan. But, in the next instant his head came up and his jaw set firmly.

"That's the best news I've heard in a long time," he said aloud, talking to himself as he pushed through the jubilant South High crowd. "You can't beat a thing by trying to dodge it. I found that out in this game. And I'll beat this hold Bimbo's got over me if it takes three more years to do it!"

With this, Speed strode into the clubhouse, and met his downhearted team-mates, smiling. As for a certain young lady, could she have known of this new resolution, she might have been less disappointed in the game's outcome . . . and more hopeful of a certain young man's future. She might even have decided that Speed Durgan had won a victory even though he had lost.

CHAPTER VIII

THE OLD FIGHT RENEWED

A YEAR and a half sped past which seemed to a busily engaged Speed Durgan like the flicker of a second hand, once the time was gone. And, in this year and a half, he had become a loyal son of Billiter, a well known and much respected Sophomore—thanks to his athletic prowess— and sought after by the leading fraternities. Altogether his position in college was a most happy one. As pitcher on the Freshman nine, he had continued his winning ways, leading his Class team to the Class Championship, the first time a Freshman team had won the baseball title. Because of his brilliant performance on the mound it had been predicted that Speed Durgan would easily make the Varsity in his Sophomore year and perhaps prove one of the greatest pitchers in the history of the Little Valley Conference. Speed naturally hoped that he might be able to live up to these predictions. And he thrilled at being chosen by Coach Thacker as Billiter's number one twirler. Perhaps he might be able to achieve in college what he had narrowly missed realizing in high school—the handing up of an undefeated record. Of course competition was bound to be much stiffer . . . and then there was Bimbo to be considered. He had apparently created as big a sensation in Winston as he, Speed, had aroused in Billiter. Already Bimbo was being heralded as the coming new home run king of the Little Valley Conference—his style of batting being likened to Babe Ruth's. Winston, on the strength of Bimbo's showing was even counting the big game of the year with Billiter as good as won. And such optimism so early in the season had hitherto been unheard of!

Marjory Coulter, much to Speed's regret, was also a student at Winston. He knew, quite certainly, that her attending this college had been uninfluenced by the fact that Bimbo Bailey had decided to go there. But he couldn't help wishing that his friend of high school days had come to Billiter instead. Chances were, however, that she had lost patience with him . . . lost faith in his ever being able to overcome his complex. Not that she had ever actually indicated such a feeling. She had always treated him cordially and had tried to keep off the subject of South High's last victory over him when in his company. Marjory wasn't the sort who believed in crying over spilled milk. She had paid her bet by going to South High's party with Bimbo and making the best of it, although Speed sensed that she would have much preferred to be with the North High crowd. But, now, Marjory was certain to be thoroughly imbued with Winston spirit—a full-fledged rooter for Bimbo and the Winston team. There was every reason why she should be since there was no cause for her allegiance to be divided. And, while she kept in correspondence touch with Speed occasionally, her letters were strongly partisan. It was Winston this and Winston that . . . the greatest debating team . . . the greatest hockey team . . . the greatest *everything!*

"They sure sell Winston to the outside world!" Speed had grinned, after reading one of Marjory's enthusiastic ravings. "I'll have to look that college over when we go there to play our big game this year. If I took her writings seriously she'd have me believing I'd picked the wrong school!"

Jerry Martin, Speed's room-mate, star second sacker and influential member of the Three Arts Club, was the peppiest, busiest man on the campus. He found time for debating and singing in the college glee club as well—and, on occasion, had been known to make appearances at three different functions on the same evening. No one could quite figure out when Jerry did his studying—even Speed could shed no light on the matter unless his dizzy room-mate was just one of those *natural* students. The fact remained, however, that he knew enough about his lessons to get passing marks.

"I study as I run!" Jerry had explained to envious questioners. "I'm one of those 'take-advantage-of-spare-minutes' men! I got that idea from an ad once and it's always stuck with me. You can do anything you want to if you only think you can! Next year I expect to go in for a few more things as I'm finding too much time on my hands!"

"Whew!" his listeners would gasp, and stagger away, completely done up at the mere suggestion. "How does that boy stand it? He must never sleep! That's it! Hey, Speed—does Jerry ever sleep?"

"I don't know," Speed answered, quite truthfully. "He always goes to bed with a bunch of books and papers. He's got a small light rigged up at the head of his bed to work by . . . but I don't lie awake keeping tab on him. I'm usually sawing wood in a couple of minutes."

"Maybe he gets his studies in his sleep!" advanced a student who was majoring in psychology and philosophy. "The mind does funny pranks sometimes. Why don't you watch him some night with one eye open and report to us what happens? He's got us all guessing!"

Speed shook his head. "Nope—that's past my working hours. What Jerry does after I go to bed is his business, not mine. My brain shop is closed for the day."

"But you wouldn't even do this in the interest of science?" persisted the psychological nut.

"I wouldn't even do it if you paid me for it!" was Speed's retort.

"Then it looks like we'd have to keep on cramming," was the student's despondent reply, "when if we could just discover Jerry's study secret, college life would be one sweet song!"

"Speed," addressed Billiter's miracle man one day in mid-season. "I've just about decided that you're a pretty fair pitcher."

"You have?" smiled Speed, "What took you so long?"

"I always play safe. Besides, a fellow's apt to be partial to a room-mate. But something happened today which convinced me that you're the berries!"

Speed stared at Jerry curiously.

"I'll bite—what was it?"

"There's a guy in college who's a dead ringer for you! He's a Freshman by the name of Ronald Cooper. Ever hear of him?"

"No. I've left my Freshman days behind me."

"Well, I was rushing across the campus and when I spotted this guy Cooper I thought he was you."

"No kidding?"

"Straight dope! You know what a hurry I'm usually in? But the suit this Cooper was wearing stopped me—since I'd never seen it on you. Besides—you were wearing spats!"

"Me—wearing *spats?*" Speed made a playful gesture at cuffing his room-mate.

"So I said to this apparition which I thought was you— 'well, Speed, I never thought you'd come to this!' And the ghost smiled and said, in a high falsetto voice, 'Thanks so much for the compliment!' . . . Of course, I knew right then that either I was goofy or it was a case of mistaken identity!"

"I hope you would!"

"So I asked for an introduction and after we'd exchanged names, Freshie boasted about his resembling you. It seems he's really crazy about sports but his mother would never let him play anything more violent than checkers. He's one of the sort that carries a pair of rubbers wrapped up in a piece of brown paper for fear he'd be caught out in a sudden rain far from home! Means well, you understand, but too much home complex!"

"I get you!" nodded Speed, his face flushing. He didn't like the word 'complex' used about anybody.

"Ronnie—that's what he wants me to call him—well, Ronnie told me he'd give his right arm to meet you. Just like that—you could cut his right arm off at the shoulder with a butcher's meat cleaver—honest, you've no idea how crazy this bird is about you! He's gone to all the games and has actually cheered his vocal chords raw over your pitching. Then he goes home, after your victory, and looks himself in the glass and pats himself on the chest and tells himself, "Good work, old boy. You saved the day again!"

Speed was laughing heartily now.

"Jerry, you're making that stuff up. It's a riot!"

"Wait till you meet this bozo and judge for yourself!" rejoined the busiest man in college. "I made an appointment for him to meet us at the dorm at seven-thirty tonight. I had to cancel two meetings to do it but he's the biggest scream I've ever bumped into. And when you see him, outside of his fussy way of dressing, you're going to feel like you're looking in the mirror at yourself!"

"If a guy like you describe looks like me, or I look like him, I'm going to jump out the window and end it all!" declared Speed, humorously.

"Wait! I only wish I had a double on the campus. Think of all the uses he could be put to. I could wish him off on all the boresome affairs I didn't care to attend, get him to appear at classes for me and have him wait at the tailor's while the only suit I own was being pressed!"

"What would you be doing, meanwhile?"

"I'd be waiting in the bathtub, drinking hot chocolate and getting warmed up on my glee club program!"

"Be serious, Jerry! What's your idea wishing this adoring Freshie on me? I have my own troubles!"

"One thing—I didn't have the heart to turn the hero worshipper down. Second—the resemblance was so darn striking that I wanted to see you two together. Third—I felt kind of sorry for the poor dub. He acted so flattered to be mistaken for you that I thought I'd put him next so he could get some idea of the real thing and put on an honest-to-goodness imitation after this!"

"Thanks!" grinned Speed. "But how did all this convince you that I was a pretty fair pitcher?"

"Why, by the simple process of inductive reasoning. If you hadn't been a pretty fair pitcher I'd have insulted the esteemed Mr. Cooper by mistaking him for you!"

"I see!" rejoined Speed, much amused. "That's a new way of forming an opinion about people. Rather round about but I can appreciate its . . . er . . . decided merits!"

"Now, listen!" demanded Jerry, clutching Speed's arm. "I'll give you the real low-down on why I'm putting you next to Ronnie! We need someone to run errands for us . . . and to take care of our room! Neither of us can afford to hire it done . . . and this boy, Ronnie, will be tickled silly to do it for us—just to be paid off on reflected glory!"

"Oh ho!" exclaimed Speed. "Now I get you! You old schemer! That makes me suspicious! How do I know but what you've got a bunch of Freshies all organized, doing your studying for you and giving you the dope in a nutshell so you can spill it at classes? Let's see your notebooks! Let's see if they're in your own handwriting!"

"Sssh! Don't give me away!" joshed Jerry.

"But we're living in the age of efficiency and when there's so many worthwhile things to be doing, why load up your life with trifles .. ... especially when there are others who just love to do trifling things?"

"The master mind at work!" kidded Speed. "All right—I'll meet my dizzy double but I leave it to you to do the bargaining. If you can land him as our chief cook, bottle washer and valet, more power to you!"

That evening, as it neared seven-thirty, Speed Durgan closed his study books and sat regarding his dynamic room-mate who was going over the points on a debate and a play that the Three Arts Club was considering producing. Jerry was a character! He certainly made life interesting for everybody with whom he came in contact. And this Ronnie business. . . ! Speed was half sorry now that he'd even consented to see the fellow. The thoughts of being held up as an idol by anybody made him feel uncomfortable. This Ronnie person must be rather simple. It seemed a shame to be playing on his credulity. Jerry had a way of making folks believe most anything. No telling what he'd pull on the poor, unsuspecting Freshie! At the moment, however, Jerry's mind seemed miles away. He had a peculiar ability to detach himself from a subject and come back to it with amazing swiftness, taking up exactly where he had left off with the same enthusiasm. And this is what Jerry did now, when a hesitant rap sounded on the door.

"There's your twin brother!" he cried, pushing debate papers and play aside to jump for the door. "Get ready, Speed, to meet yourself coming in!"

Speed stood up, looking toward the door with great, natural curiosity.

"Hel-lo, Ronnie!" greeted Jerry with unmistakeable cordiality, to a figure which stood in the hallway. "Step right in, sir! Step right in!"

"Oh! Thank you. I . . . !"

"It's quite all right, Mr. Cooper, I want you to meet the one and only Mr. Speed Durgan, even though, to see you both, I'd swear there were two!"

Speed advanced with outstretched hand.

"Jerry's told me about his mistaking you for

me," he said, noting the visitor's embarrass-
ment. "Let me offer you my sympathy and my
apology!"

"Oh, not at all! As I told Mr. Martin, I was
really terribly flattered! And it's not the first
time I've been taken for you, either, so there
must be something to our looking alike. I'm
surer than ever now that I've seen you up close!"

"Funny thing!" chuckled Jerry, sizing up
Ronnie and Speed. "I can't tell which one of
you looks like the other. Speed, what do you
think of the resemblance?"

"I must say it's most remarkable!" declared
Billiter's new pitching sensation impressed.
"You could take my place on the mound, Mr.
Cooper, and nobody'd know the difference!"

"Perhaps not!" conceded the Freshman,
pleased. "Not, at any rate, till I threw the first
ball!"

Jerry winked at Speed who gestured, gravely.

"Have you ever played the game, Mr.
Cooper?"

"I wish you'd call me Ronnie. It makes me
feel funny to be called Cooper. No. I've never
played baseball. Oh, I've played catch some but

my folks . . . . my mother, she was very nervous. She said she'd rather I didn't. But I understand all about it and I attend the games. I get a big kick out of watching you pitch . . . especially since folks say I look so much like you! I hope you don't mind?"

"That you look like me?" laughed Speed. "Why, no—I don't suppose you could help that."

"Well, I don't know as I would try if I could. You see, I've always wanted to go in for sports but my folks . . . I mean, mother . . . . she . . . "

"Yes, we get you!" broke in Jerry, "Your mother's had quite an effect on your life. Too bad she didn't realize that a fellow who looked like you was really cut out for a baseball pitcher. You can prove it to her now—what you should have been—by taking Speed home and showing her!"

"Oh, I'd be very happy to. Maybe he could come home with me Spring vacation. Would you care to do that, Mr. Durgan?"

"Never mind the Durgan," said Speed, amused at the Freshie's gullibility. "I'm sorry but my spring vacation plans are all made."

"See here, Ronnie," spoke Jerry, with a wise look at Speed. "It's just possible that you may be able to render a great service to us . . . I mean—to Speed."

"Me? Service?" repeated the Freshman, eagerly. "Why, I'd be glad to do anything . . . I'd consider it an honor. . . !"

"Just so—and it *would* be an honor, too, because Speed Durgan, at the end of this season, is going to be proclaimed as the greatest pitcher in the history of old Billiter. It's going to mean something to be able to say that you know him! You—a Freshman! There's lots of fellows who would jump at the chance that's yours!"

Speed, unable to keep his face straight, had turned toward the window. Jerry certainly was spreading it on thick . . . and Ronnie seemed to be swallowing it whole. Oh, well—Freshies were supposed to fall hard and innocently for most propositions.

"But I don't know as I can stand another guy who looks like myself around!" Speed was thinking.

"In what way could I be of service?" asked Ronnie, face glowing. "All you have to do is say the word!"

"Well, now, Ronnie—that's fine! That's magnanimous of you! That's real Billiter spirit! We've each of us got to serve a purpose. Me, for instance! While it happens that I'm also on the team, I realize that my position isn't nearly so important as that of Speed. If Billiter is to play through an undefeated season this year, it all rests mainly on his shoulders! That being the case, it behooves us to save Speed all we can . . . . to take from him all the burdens possible . . . to make his moments off the diamond free of strain . . . help him to preserve that mental and physical attitude so necessary to his brand of pitching. Do you understand?"

"Why, I . . . I think I'm beginning to!" gasped the fellow who looked like Billiter's number one pitcher.

Speed winced, concentrating his attention upon something of apparent great interest out the window.

"Then," continued Jerry, unblushingly, "all you've got to do is to volunteer as Speed's man Friday. Drop in here each day and do such odd jobs as he may have for you. Straighten up the room, take his spare suit to be pressed, get books for him from the library, and so forth and so on! Get the idea?"

Speed turned from the window, unable to resist seeing how Ronnie might be taking this bald proposal. But what he saw struck him as more pathetic than humorous. There was a look of almost ecstacy on the Freshman's face—a look which said plainer than words that he considered himself the most favored of Billiter men.

"When can I begin?" was Ronnie's response. "Is there something that I can do for you tonight, Mr. Durgan . . . I . . . er . . . mean—Speed? Say—I can't tell you how much I appreciate this—the chance to be near you fellows. I've been sort of alone since I came here and I . . . well, I guess I haven't been active enough. A fellow's got to be doing something to get noticed . . . and I certainly want to do my part."

"You're on the right track now," assured Jerry. "You stick with us and you'll meet the best guys in college. Of course you've always got to remember your place. A Freshie is mostly to be seen and not heard. Speak when spoken

(102)

to, otherwise keep silent and look wise. You'll make a bigger hit that way—otherwise you may *get* hit. That's just a tip. And here's something else. We . . . er . . . don't want to bother Speed any more than we can help so I . . . er . . . I'll give you quite a few of the hints as to what to do around here."

"I—I see. We'll sort of work together," grasped Ronnie.

"No, not exactly. You'll do the work, but . . . that is . . ." Jerry looked momentarily distressed. "You see, I'm extremely busy myself. In fact, there's three places I ought to be right this minute besides here. But, up to now, I've been . . . er . . . trying to do my bit by Speed, too. It's just too much, however—entirely too much. As a consequence I've neglected some of my own personal matters."

"And you'd like me to help you, too?" divined Ronnie. "Well, if I have any time left after serving Speed, I . . . !"

Ronnie looked toward Speed, wonderingly.

"I'll try not to take up too much of your time," Speed rejoined, smiling.

"Ronnie, you're a man after my own heart!"

declared Jerry, impressively. "I've never met a Freshman like you! I'm sure we're going to get along famously—famously! Now, if you don't mind I'll run along to the Three Arts Club. I've a committee meeting there if the members haven't gotten sore waiting and gone home . . . !"

"Oh, Mr. Martin . . . or rather, Jerry! Are you a member of the Three Arts Club?" exclaimed Ronnie, enviously. "Oh, that must be marvelous to belong to that organization! I'd give anything in the world if I . . . it's been one of my secret ambitions . . . I'm very much interested in artistic things—the stage . . . !"

Ronnie seemed lost in a confusion of words, trying to express his pent-up feelings.

"Really?" replied Jerry, at the door, flashing Speed a look which, translated into language, said: "Wouldn't that *kill* you?"

"I suppose you know, Ronnie," reminded Speed, "that a Freshman isn't eligible for membership!"

"Oh, yes—I know that!" nodded Ronnie. "But next year . . . ?"

"Of course," said Jerry, "if a Freshman does

something distinctive his first year, he might win the honor of being pledged while still a Freshman and be taken in at the first meeting of his Sophomore term. We'll have to talk about that, Ronnie, when I have more time!"

"Yes, yes! I'd be glad to!" said Ronnie, all but overwhelmed.

"Well, good night! I'll see you again to-morrow. You're under Speed's orders now!"

And with this, the industrious Jerry was gone, leaving the two fellows who looked alike, together.

"Jerry's a . . . a wonderful fellow, isn't he?" breathed Ronnie, turning to Speed. "I—I'm certainly grateful to him . . . and to you! I'll try to show you how much I appreciate . . ."

"That's all right, Ronnie," said Speed, in an endeavor to put the much flustered Freshman at his ease. "I don't happen to have anything you can do for me tonight. Got your studies for to-morrow?"

"Yes, sir . . . yes, I have. Getting back to my looking like you—isn't it funny, Speed, that two people could look so much alike and yet be so different?" There was something almost wistful in the question.

"Well, in a way I suppose it is," Speed admitted, studying Ronnie intently.

"I've wanted to take part in sports. I've got the build for it. When I was younger I was rather sickly and mother was afraid. Now I feel backward about it and I guess the fellows think I'm scared to go out! But that's not the reason . . . I just don't have the talent. I feel that everyone's superior to me. Did you ever have that feeling?"

Speed looked off into space, face sobering.

"Not quite that bad," he said, softly. "There's only one guy that I ever felt was superior . . . and he's come pretty close to ruining my peace of mind!"

"But you've overcome that feeling now, haven't you?" asked an admiring Ronnie.

Speed shook his head. "It still bothers me," he admitted, at the risk of crumbling an idol before his worshipper's feet. "But I'm fighting it!"

Ronnie sat for a moment, gazing sympathetically at him whom he had volunteered to serve.

"It's a terrible thing to fight," he murmured,

finally. "Maybe we're not so different after all?"

"Maybe we're not," agreed Speed, huskily, and a flash of understanding passed between the two.

CHAPTER IX

STRANGE THINGS HAPPEN

WITH the baseball season two-thirds over and Billiter and Winston Colleges still riding the victory crest, sports writers began to predict that the contest between these two rivals would, barring an upset, decide the Little Valley Conference championship.

"Great pitching by Speed Durgan and great hitting by Bimbo Bailey have been the two outstanding factors in the triumphant campaign waged by Billiter and Winston," one newspaper declared. "Durgan is as effective a hurler as has been seen in the Conference, he narrowly having missed two no-hit games this season. In the game against Tremper, Speed had to retire but two more batters to enter the hall of fame but fate decreed against him when a slow rolling ball, hit down to short, was beat to first by an eyelash. Most of Billiter's wins this year have been by top-heavy scores simply because the opposition has been held so helpless. Winston, on the other hand, with fair pitching, is being supported by terrific hitting with Bimbo Bailey flailing the ball on his way to a new home run record. The Conference record is thirteen and Bimbo already has nine with five games yet to play."

Strangely enough, as the season had progressed toward the climaxing game of the season with Winston, a nervous condition had been observed to be coming upon Speed Durgan. This condition had been most noticeable at the training table where his loss of appetite had come to the immediate attention of the coach.

"What's the matter, Speed? Not feeling well?" Coach Thacker inquired, anxiously.

"Okay," was Speed's response. "Just not overly hungry, that's all."

"You want to feed well," the Coach advised. "It's pretty hard to pitch a stiff game of ball on an empty stomach. You need plenty of nourishment to give you vitality."

"I can't eat if the food doesn't appeal to me," Speed objected. "If I do, it's like lead in my stomach."

"You're just getting tired of training table grub!" the Coach decided. "I'll have the Chef give you more variety."

But a greater selection of dishes did not seem to materially affect Speed's lost appetite. Moreover, he commenced to start at sudden noises. One night he jerked so that he spilled his coffee when first baseman Dan Lawrence let an unexpected whoop out of him.

"Hold it!" team-mates grinned.

"Right on my trouser leg!" moaned catcher Ed Keller, who sat next to Speed. "Say, guys— is coffee stain permanent? If it is—Speed owes me a new pair of pants. I think my leg's burned, too, the way it feels. Boy—it's getting so it's dangerous to sit near him!"

"I'm darn sorry," apologized Speed. "I don't know why I jumped then."

"And I don't know why I *didn't* jump!" rejoined Ed. "I saw that spout of coffee coming my way and I sat here petrified and let it land. Good grief—this pant leg must have soaked up half a cup!"

"Just exactly!" measured Speed, examining the coffee still left in his cup.

The fellows at the training table howled.

"Speed's developing a bad case of nerves," Jerry Martin confided gravely to shortstop Bert

Carver. "I'm his room-mate. I ought to know."

"But do you know what's causing it?" asked Bert.

Jerry shook his head. "That's got me stumped. I've been so busy I haven't had a chance to do any detective work. I quizzed Ronnie—that's our Fresh-man Friday . . . but he didn't seem to have an idea although he admitted he'd been worrying about Speed for several weeks. Something's got under his skin, that's a cinch."

"Maybe it's a germ of some kind," suggested Bert, half-humorously. "No kidding, though, something's got to be done about this! If Speed should go up in smoke we might as well kiss goodbye to our championship hopes!"

"You said it!" agreed Jerry. "I'll just have to take time off from one activity or another and get to the bottom of this! I've got one lead to start on. Every Sunday morning since the beginning of the season, Speed's been receiving a special delivery letter from somewhere that's apparently irritated him greatly. I figured it was from some girl and, since he's never said anything to me about it, I haven't tried to make it any of my business. But maybe these letters have some connection. Anyhow, I'm going to do some investigating!"

"I would if I was you!" encouraged Bert. "And if you find it's a girl that's been causing the trouble, she ought to be shot!"

"Well . . . er . . . scolded at any rate!" modified Jerry. "I'll report back later!"

Returning to his room ahead of Speed some evenings later, Jerry decided that the time was propitious for him to determine what he could that might be contributing to his room-mate's nervousness.

"I hate to do this," he told himself, "but I've got to go through Speed's desk. That's where I'm apt to find the evidence!"

It seemed like a sneaky thing to do but Jerry assured himself that it was for a good cause. But one more game remained on Billiter's schedule before the all-important Winston game and Speed Durgan had been slipping fast. In the last encounter he had lost a five run lead as late as the seventh inning and had just staggered through to win, eight to six. The newspapers had been lenient, stating that Speed had suffered an off day, but those on the inside knew better. Speed's morale was gradually being undermined and at a time when his services were needed most.

"Coach Thacker is about crazy," thought Jerry, as he rummaged through the desk, taking care to replace everything as nearly as he could in the exact position he had found it. "Speed's condition is beginning to upset the team, too. And if the fellows once get shaky behind him— good night!"

Jerry's search was specifically for one or more of the special delivery letters. he felt, instinctively, that these would throw some light on the mystery. But Speed had apparently taken care to hide them well—if he had not destroyed them.

"Hello! This drawer's locked!" discovered Jerry. "I'll bet they're in here!" He debated a moment. "I could open this with my pen knife but how to get it closed again? . . . Oh, well —here's taking a chance!"

It was the work of a minute to pry the drawer open and Jerry whistled his joy at coming upon the packet of special delivery letters he was seeking.

"Doesn't look like a girl's hand," he observed. "But you never can tell . . . . !"

A guilty feeling came over him as he took the letters up and removed the rubber band about them. It hardly seemed right to be delving into Speed's private affairs, regardless of the justification. And then, too, Speed was apt to be coming in any minute! . . . Jerry left the drawer in such a position that he could slip the letters in and push it shut in an instant.

"I'll look at the last letter which is on top," he decided, "and if it doesn't appear to have any connection, I'll quit."

A second glance at the envelope, however, caused him to exclaim in surprise.

"Hello! It's postmarked "Winston"! That's interesting!"

A single sheet of paper was inside. On this sheet, typed in capital letters, was the following:

HOME RUN NUMBER "11" TODAY ALSO HIT TWO SINGLES AND A THREE BAGGER . . . JUST GETING WARMED UP FOR OUR LITTLE ANNUAL MEETING!

BIMBO

"Holy smoke!" gasped Jerry. "So this is what has been going on! Well, Coach Thacker's got to hear of this—at once!"

There was the sound of a doorknob turning. Jerry slipped the sheet back in the envelope, having no time to place the rubber band about the packet. In almost one movement he dropped the letters in the drawer and was in the act of sliding it shut when he knew that the door had been opened and that he was being watched.

"Might as well face the music!" Jerry thought, and whirled. "Oh, well . . . hello, Ronnie! I . . . er . . . wasn't expecting you . . . come right in! Come right in! . . . Going to pick up around here, are you? That's fine!"

Jerry could not conceal his relief even though he could see that Ronnie was staring at him suspiciously. The Freshman, Jerry decided, wasn't *too* dumb. Ronnie knew that Jerry was seated at Speed's desk and he indicated that he knew it in the first thing that he said.

"You—you were expecting *Speed?*"

"Well, yes—I figured he was due to be along any minute! You're a little earlier tonight, aren't you?"

"Yes. I'm going out tonight. Got to take in a lecture. Was there anything special you wanted?"

"Let me see . . . . let me see! Not that I think of at the moment. Oh . . . er . . . yes! Speed's tuxedo needs pressing—mine, too. Can you take 'em down to the tailors?"

"I guess so," said Ronnie, with a glance toward the desk. He moved toward the closet and presently emerged with the garments. "Should I come back tonight?"

"Why . . . er . . . if you've something else on . . . I don't think we'll be needing you. Let the room go till tomorrow. We've lived in it a lot worse than this," said Jerry, lamely.

"Just as you say!" nodded Ronnie, soberly, and vanished into the hall after another questioning glance at Speed's desk.

"Whew!" breathed Jerry, as Ronnie was gone. "What a narrow escape! That baby not only looks like Speed now, but he's grown to love him like a twin brother. And if he'd caught me red-handed . . . .! I wonder just how much he saw, anyway?"

Jerry pulled the drawer open again with the

intention of re-arranging the letters but he was again arrested by the sound of the doorknob turning.

"Now, what?" he muttered, shutting the drawer, quickly, and moving away from the desk.

"See here, Jerry!" demanded the angry voice of Speed. "I met Ronnie on the stairs. What do you mean sending him out with my tuxedo? It doesn't need pressing! I just had it pressed day before yesterday!"

"You did? It doesn't" exclaimed Jerry, confused. "Well, I . . . excuse me! It didn't look very pressed to me!"

"It's perfectly pressed!" declared Speed, holding the tuxedo up for a blank-faced Jerry to examine. "See for yourself!"

Jerry grinned sheepishly and scratched his head. "Do you know what I must have done?" he said. "I must have picked my tuxedo up and looked at it twice . . . and thought one of the times that it was yours!"

"You're goofy!" reproved Speed, placing his tuxedo gently back on a hanger. "After this I'll give Ronnie orders for things I want done.

Besides, while we're on the subject, I want you to lay off the way you're treating Ronnie. He's a darn nice fellow and you're not going to be running his legs off all the time!"

Jerry stiffened. He was not prepared for this outburst. Here was a new show of temperament, or nervousness or what have you?

"Yeah? Who's running the little boy's legs off? He's getting a kick out of it, isn't he? Look at the big times he's in on! Hanging around when the gang is here—soaking up atmosphere —rubbing elbows with the upper classmen. There's not a Freshman on the campus wouldn't give his eye teeth to trade places with him . . . and Ronnie knows it. Why get so sentimental all of a sudden?"

"Because I resent the way you've got him trained! 'Sir-ing' all the boys and taking orders like a Chinese coolie. The boys get a big laugh out of it, of course. But I wouldn't take orders like that from anybody. I wouldn't bow down and humble myself before my equals. It's bad training for Ronnie. He feels inferior enough to the rest of us as it is!"

"He *is* inferior!" declared Jerry. "He's a

poor thing and we're handing him crumbs that
he thinks are diamonds?"

"All right—but we know they're NOT diamonds, don't we?" rejoined Speed, feelingly.
"We know it's just the bunk! We know that
Ronnie's been sold to the eyebrows on reflected
glory stuff! That we've just been stringing him
along! And I, for one, am putting my foot
down. I'm sick and disgusted of the whole business. Can you imagine how I feel, seeing a guy
foot-padding it around who's the dead image
of me—taking orders from you like a lord?
Where do you get off, pulling these high-
handed airs? You put over something pretty
smart and it's gone to your head! But from now
on this whole business stops!"

"You mean . . . ?" said Jerry, after a breathless moment. "That ..... er ..... Ronnie leaves
our employ?"

The query sounded ludicrous.

"If you put it that way—yes!" snapped
Speed. "I believe in every fellow being free
. . . in not being dominated by anybody! .....
Anybody, understand?"

Jerry gazed at Speed steadily as a certain

something occurred to him—like putting two and two together. "Yes," he said, meaningfully. "I think I understand!"

With that he grabbed up his cap and strode from the room, bound for Coach Thacker's office.

"I'd like to have a look at those letters," the Coach said, after listening to the astounding story that Speed's room-mate had to tell.

"Well, the only way you could work it would be to come to the room some time when Speed is away," proposed Jerry. "I'm hoping he doesn't go to that drawer again until next Sunday morning when he'll probably get the last one of these *love* letters since next Saturday will be the last game Bimbo plays in before his team meets us!"

"And when he goes to the drawer you feel he's bound to know it's been tampered with?"

"Yes, because I pried it open and I can't get it back exactly as it was unless I had the key— which he carries on his key ring. Ordinarily I'd try to unlock and lock the drawer after he goes to bed, by taking the key from the pocket of his trousers, but Speed's been sleeping so lightly lately that the least little sound has him wide awake! I'd be caught sure as shooting!"

"He's apparently very sensitive about this," deduced Coach Thacker, "or he certainly would have said something to you about it. It's a question what his reaction is going to be if he finds that someone has been into his drawer."

"I've got it!" cried Jerry. "I can stage a fake robbery—scatter stuff around the room—have a few of my things missing as well as his—and let him walk in on it! That'll keep him from suspecting!"

Coach Thacker considered the suggestion a long time. "It's a pretty heroic procedure," he said, finally. "A robbery scare isn't a good advertisement for the college. But we may be able to handle this in a way to avoid publicity. I'll take the office into confidence on this and you advise Speed to say nothing as it looks like an inside job . . . some student's work. Let him report the theft to the office for a secret investigation."

"Okay" said Jerry. "Meanwhile, do you still want to have a look at those letters?"

"Not only a look," said Coach Thacker, "But, under this plan—I *want* the letters!"

When Ronnie Cooper came over to the room the following day he found Speed waiting for him.

"I want to have a talk with you," Speed told him, and his Freshman admirer could sense at once that it was about something unpleasant.

"What's the matter? he asked, concernedly. "Did I pull some bonehead?"

"No," said Speed, coming directly to the point. "But Jerry and I have been treating you rotten . . . we played you for a . . . a sucker . . . and you . . you took the hook—bait, line and sinker!"

"I—I don't believe I understand," said Ronnie, painfully.

"No, you wouldn't," replied Speed. "You're so darn trusting that you figure nobody would take advantage of you. But that's all boloney, Ronnie. This making you a handy man wasn't my idea. I can at least say that much. But I let Jerry put it over so I'm partly to blame. But I'm calling a halt to it right now."

The fellow who strikingly resembled Billiter's pitching ace stared in open-mouthed wonderment.

"Why, why—I haven't minded doing these things for you fellows, Speed. It's all right. You don't need to feel badly about it—if that's what you mean."

"It's not that . . . but it's bad for you, Ronnie. I've been thinking it over. You shouldn't knuckle under to anyone. Service is a fine thing but it must be on an equal basis. Jerry and I have been making a—a doormat out of you . . . and that isn't right. It—it robs a fellow of his self-respect."

Ronnie looked troubled.

"Then—then you don't want me to help you any more?"

"I'd rather you wouldn't. I'd feel better about it. While most of the fellows think it's a huge joke . . . I hope you won't be too hurt at this, Ronnie . . . I don't think it's a joke at all."

"Oh, I can stand being laughed at. I'm used to that," Ronnie replied, spiritedly. "And I really was getting a lot of fun out of what I was doing! I'd miss seeing you fellows if I had to quit—honest!"

Speed, not having anticipated this reaction, found himself perplexed but none the less adamant.

"Well, there's nothing to prevent your dropping over occasionally for a visit," he answered. "And if I can ever do anything for you I'll be more than glad."

"You've already done a lot for me," said Ronnie, gratefully. "More than you realize. You fellows may have used me for a servant but you gave me an opportunity to rub shoulders with the finest fellows in college . . . . and to wear off a good deal of my inferiority complex."

Speed started, surprised.

"How's that?"

"Why—because I've found out that the fellows I felt were superior to me aren't so much different. They have their own problems and their own weaknesses to fight against just like I have."

"If you've learned that, you've learned a lot," said Speed, extending his hand. "Goodbye, Ronnie. You've got good stuff in you and, one of these days, you're going to cash in on it!"

"I hope so," replied Ronnie, taking Speed's hand, "And if I do it's going to be, not only because I look like you, but because I've started *acting* like you!"

"If you knew me better," said Speed, his face burning. "You wouldn't say that. But I appreciate your faith in me—just the same!"

Billiter College stayed in the running for the Conference Championship by triumphing over Slater University in a free-hitting game by the score of 11 to 7, with Speed Durgan, her ace, apparently taking it easy in the box. Twice Billiter came from behind to overcome Slater leads but, in the later innings, Speed Durgan put on pressure to quell further rallies and make the game safe for his team.

"Pretty rocky going!" was the opinion of worried Billiter fans following the contest. "They can say Speed let down if they want to but he's not the same pitcher he was earlier in the season. He'd better be in top form next Saturday running up against that Winston outfit of sluggers. A good defensive team would have finished us today on the runs Speed spotted Slater. No question about it—Speed's a great pitcher—but he can't afford to slow up now. Don't you believe the report that he's doing it to save his arm—there's some other reason!"

"Playing Winston on their home diamond

is against us, too!" declared a veteran rooter. "They say that short right field fence is just made for Bimbo's home runs!"

"Say—I'd like to see that fellow play!" remarked another. "What's this story going the rounds that he came from the same town as Speed did? Too bad he didn't come to Billiter, too! Then we'd have nothing to worry about!"

Returning to his room after the game and arriving ahead of Jerry, one Speed Durgan was shocked to find that the room had been entered. There were papers and clothing strewn about the floor as though the thief had been in great haste. Both Jerry's and his desk had been gone through and private drawers opened. A sudden fear seized Speed. Looking in the drawer which he had kept locked, his fear was realized at discovery that the packet of special delivery letters was missing. There were other things missing, too—some change, stamps, a watch charm, a pen knife—all small articles that a person could have carried away without detection.

"But what could anyone want with those letters?" an agonized Speed wondered. "Unless he might have thought there was something valuable in them!"

Jerry, hurrying in, stopped in the doorway and exclaimed in surprise.

"What the dickens you doing? Going on a tear? This room is a sight! . . . Boy, you'd better page Ronnie right away!"

"Listen, Jerry—we've been robbed!" cried Speed. "I just got in! This room's just as I found it!"

"Robbed!" cried Jerry, hoping that his pretended concern seemed real. "You don't mean it —not in broad daylight? A sneak thief, eh? What's missing?"

"I haven't checked up closely yet," answered Speed. "Most important thing so far is a bunch of . . . er . ... . papers I kept in that little drawer!"

"That so? . ... . Hey—my desk's been ransacked, too! What do you know about this? If I ever catch the guy who pulled this job I'll bust his face!"

The two room-mates spent several frenzied minutes determining the extent of their losses.

"Well, I didn't lose so much," declared Jerry, with a sigh of relief. "A diamond stick pin, some cuff links, a couple of dollars I'd left to pay for my laundry, and a second-hand watch!"

"Whoever broke in here was evidently scared away before he got a chance to take much," decided Speed. "But I'd like to get those papers back!"

"What papers were they?"

"A . . . just something personal. No earthly use to anyone else."

"I'm lucky that way. I don't have any valuable papers. But we'd better make a list of our losses and report this theft to the office. Say— where's Ronnie? He's usually here Saturday afternoons after the game! He's got a pass key and . . . . !"

Speed started. "That's so, he has! I forgot to ask him for it."

"What do you mean?"

"Why, Ronnie's not coming here any more —I told him we could do without his services."

Jerry shook his head, mournfully. "You might at least have let him work the week out. Now *we've* got to clean up this mess!"

"You don't suppose Ronnie could have lost the pass key and someone used it to get in here, do you?" speculated Speed.

"Now there's an idea!" exclaimed Jerry, glancing at Speed shrewdly. "This looks like an inside job to me . . . like some student had pulled it. You know, we'd better be pretty close-mouthed about this until the thief is tracked down or suspicion may rest on the wrong party. Was the door locked when you came in?"

Speed nodded, thoughtfully. "Yes, it was locked. I'd better get in touch with Ronnie."

"All right—you check up on that key he's got and I'll go down to the office and tell 'em about this," said Jerry. "Otherwise, mum's the word, don't you think?"

"Yes—there's no sense in making a sensation out of this—not unless we find other rooms have been entered, too!" said Speed, soberly.

"Great!" said Jerry, exultantly, under his breath. "Everything's worked out swell! As a sneak thief, I'm a professional. And imagine my telling Speed that if I caught the guy who did this—I'd bust his face!"

CHAPTER X

A LAMB FOR THE SLAUGHTER

DETECTIVE HALL, police authority at Billiter College, investigated the reported robbing of the room occupied by Speed Durgan and Jerry Martin. If his investigation developed any clues, Mr. Hall did not disclose them. He examined the disordered room with occasional grunts and "ahems" and left after bestowing a guarded but wise look upon Jerry.

Sunday morning the peace and quiet of the same room was broken by a familiar rap at the door.

"There's your weekly special delivery letter!" announced Jerry, sleepily, as Speed sprang out of bed as though he had been lying awake expecting it. "What you so nervous about? Great cats!"

Jerry, rubbing the sleep from his eyes, watched Speed as he crossed to the door in his bare feet.

"Special delivery for Mr. Speed Durgan," said the postman. "Sign here, please!"

A hand shoved in a piece of paper and the stub of a pencil. Speed took them and scribbled his name with nervous agitation.

"Thanks!" he snapped, taking the letter in exchange for the slip, then slamming the door.

Jerry, raised up on an elbow, could conceal his curiosity no longer.

"For the love of Mike, Speed—what's going on? These darn special deliveries every Sunday morning are getting my goat, too!"

"Who said they're getting anybody's goat?" retorted Speed, quickly.

"Well, you don't act happy over receiving 'em!" flashed Jerry. "And I'm getting tired being waked up at six o'clock on a day when I like to sleep late. I'm on the go enough during the week!"

"It's too bad about you!" growled Speed, ripping the envelope open.

"Say!" exclaimed Jerry, with great pretended innocence. "Was it these letters that were stolen yesterday? Were they the *papers* that you ... ?"

Speed, nerves on edge, turned exasperatedly upon his room-mate. "Oh, shut up, won't you? I attend to my own business—you attend to yours!"

Whereupon Jerry, with a mocking gesture of fright, stuck his head under the covers.

Monday morning, Billiter's star pitcher was notified after one of his classes that Coach Thacker wanted to see him—very important. Wondering what could be up, Speed went to the Coach's office his first free hour.

"You send for me?" he asked.

"Yes. Còme in and close the door, won't you? . . . Sit down!"

Speed did as directed, his curiosity further aroused by the evident secrecy.

"The thief who entered your room has been apprehended," Coach Thacker announced.

"You—you know about it?" gasped Speed. "Why, I—I thought . . . !"

"The matter was called to my attention due to the nature of the loot recovered," Coach Thacker explained, watching Speed's face closely.

"Oh! I—I see!" faltered Billiter's star pitcher. "Then you have the—the letters?"

"I do," said the Coach, taking them from his desk, together with the other small articles. "You must pardon me for reading them, Speed.

They were of peculiar interest to me. Quite possibly this robbery has served a very useful purpose. I've been wondering for some time what has affected your pitching and this seems to be the answer."

Speed squirmed miserably in his seat. There was nothing that he could say.

"I presume, judging from the regularity with which these notes were mailed you, that you received another one yesterday morning?" questioned the Coach.

Speed nodded and fumbled in his inside coat pocket.

"Here it is," he said. "You've seen the rest— you might as well see them all!"

Coach Thacker took up the last special delivery letter and removed the sheet of paper. He could not restrain a smile at what he read.

TWO HOMERS TODAY WHICH TIES CONFERENCE RECORD AND WATCH ME BREAK THE RECORD AGAINST YOU NEXT SATURDAY! UNTIL THEN

—BIMBO

"This Bimbo person must be quite a fellow!"

the Coach observed, dryly. "Pretty clever goat-getting campaign he's figured out. I've been checking over your record in high school again, Speed. I see the only three games you lost were annual affairs with Bimbo's team. How did these defeats happen? Were you kidded out of the games?"

"I don't think I was as effective against South Oakland as other teams," Speed admitted, reluctantly.

"And all on account of this Bimbo?" Coach Thacker pressed.

"I blame myself more than I do him!" said Speed, giving way to his pent-up feelings. "A fellow can't get another guy's goat unless he lets him! There's something about Bimbo . . . I guess it started with my being afraid of him. I don't think I'm afraid now but I still can't get away from that dominating feeling he has over me. I've been trying to fight it but he won't let me forget. He takes delight in pestering me because he knows he can! He's kept me thinking of this game with Winston all season. I knew what he was doing this for, of course, but it bothered me just the same. I couldn't throw it off. And the closer it's gotten to the game, the more I've felt it!"

Speed acted relieved at having gotten this much off his chest.

"You know what I want you to do?" spoke Coach Thacker, abruptly.

"No, sir."

"I want you to put these letters all in a big envelope and mail them back to Bimbo with a note that reads something like this: 'Save your postage. Will wire you collect after next Saturday's game to advise you that I kept you from breaking the record!'"

Speed, who had been tense with concern, relaxed sufficiently to permit a grin.

"I'd like to be able to say that—and mean it!" he replied.

"Say it a couple of times and you *will* mean it!" encouraged the Coach. "You've been accepting his suggestions so long that you believe more in what *he* tells you than you do in yourself. That's the whole trouble."

"Give me pencil and paper!" requested Speed, with sudden resolution. "Have you got a big envelope?"

"Here!" supplied the Coach. "That's the boy! You should have bounced back at Bimbo long ago."

"There!" said Speed, as he finished. "Thanks for the idea, Coach. I'd like to get back at Bimbo some way. We've been rivals for years. He's usually managed to get the upper hand. I hope I can come through against him this time or he'll be sending a telegram collect to me. He doesn't leave a stone unturned . . ."

"Well, all you've got to do is not take him seriously," counseled the Coach. "That's where you've made your mistake. Treat him as just another member of the team . . . !"

"I've tried that. It's easier said than done. Wait till you see Bimbo. He's so colorful, he stands out. And he's the best razzer that ever stepped in a coacher's box."

"As far as *you're* concerned," modified Coach Thacker. "He may not affect anyone else. Show him that he doesn't feaze you and he'll soon give up trying. Instead of glaring at him, laugh at him! Don't let him see the long face you've got in here. No wonder he rides you if you look this way!"

Speed forced a smile. "I'll be in there fighting!" he promised. "I want to beat this thing even more than you want me to. You won't let any of the team know about it, will you?"

"If the team finds out about it, it will be through you," returned Coach Thacker, significantly. "It all depends on how you face Bimbo on Saturday!"

Speed stood up. "Is that all, sir?"

"That's all. I'll mail this envelope to Bimbo for you."

"If you will, please. I . . . a . . . oh, coach. There's one thing I want to ask you. You say you caught the thief. Would you tell me who he was?"

"I'm sorry. I can't do that."

"But I . . . I think I've a right to know, sir. Can I ask you this, then—was Ronald Cooper connected in any way?"

"Cooper? . . . Cooper? . . . I don't just place him."

"He's a Freshman who—who some fellows think is a dead ringer for me. He's been coming to my room a lot lately and he could go in and out without anyone suspecting."

"I see. Well, did you have any reason to have him under suspicion?"

"N—no, except that—he had a key to the room and when I asked him for it last night he went to give it to me and then he—he said he'd lost it! Whoever got in the room did it with a key. If Ronnie had wanted to go through our things he could have done it on the quiet without littering the room . . . unless he figured that we'd be onto him more that way than if . . . !"

"But why should you think him guilty just because he claims to have lost the key?" questioned the Coach. "Wouldn't he have been more apt to have returned the key without question?"

"Understand, I—I'm not accusing him . . . but it just seems funny, that's all. I merely thought someone had gotten the key off Ronnie and done the job. The key had our room number on it."

"Forget about the whole affair!" urged the Coach. "It's all been taken care of and the fellow you mention has had nothing to do with it. Of that much I can assure you."

Speed gazed at the Coach intently as though

endeavoring to discern any tell-tale expression which would belie his words. It seemed unbelievable that Ronnie should, for any reason, have committed the act. The articles which had been taken were comparatively trivial. But there was something strange about the whole business. Just why should it happen the day after he had let Ronnie go? And why should Ronnie not be able to produce the key? Could this just have been a coincidence? And could Coach Thacker be shielding Ronnie after he, Speed, had hit upon the guilty party? These were questions for which Speed desired an answer. Coach Thacker might be ready to dismiss the entire matter but he wasn't. If it should turn out that Ronnie was at the bottom of the thing, then he would be forced to admit that he had been a poor judge of character.

"I'll quiz Ronnie on this," Speed decided. "I don't think it's an accident that those letters of mine were taken. There's something fishy about this robbery, I'll bet a hat on it!"

Jerry Martin was stopped on the campus, Tuesday afternoon, by the fellow he had originally mistaken for Speed. Ronnie Cooper appeared greatly upwrought.

"I—I've got to have a talk with you!" he gasped.

"Well, make it snappy, my ex-man Friday!" wisecracked Jerry. "I've got five engagements staring me in the face and all of them just five minutes apart. Then there's baseball practice and . . . !"

"It's about Speed!" insisted Ronnie.

"Speed? Oh!" Jerry stopped in his tracks. "Shoot!"

"I—I seem to have lost the key that you fellows gave me to your room," Ronnie explained, mournfully. "And—and Speed's holding me sort of responsible for your—your room being entered."

"He *is?*" whistled Jerry. "I didn't think he was going to say anything about that!"

"Wh—what do you mean—s—suspecting me?" Ronnie looked greatly concerned.

"No—about our room being entered," said Jerry. "It didn't amount to much. I don't see why he's making so much fuss about it!"

"Well, I—of course it's possible that someone may have picked up the ring that I carried," admitted Ronnie. "But it hurts me to feel that Speed thinks I might . . . ."

"Sure—I know!" cut in Jerry. "Excuse me if I keep walking, won't you? I've got to get where I'm going on time. Do you want to walk back this way with me? What do you want me to do—bawl Speed out?"

"N—no," faltered Ronnie. "I—I just wanted to ask you a—a question!"

"All right—let her fly. I just passed one examination today."

"I hope you won't get mad at what I'm going to ask you."

"I hope I don't, either. What is it?"

"Well, the day before someone got in your room, I—I didn't mean to see it—but what were you doing at Speed's desk?"

Jerry stopped short again. His face went red; for a moment he was speechless, then he blurted: "See here—what you trying to do— make me out the thief?"

"You were in the drawer Speed always kept locked!" replied Ronnie, with surprising courage. "You sent me out with Speed's and your tuxedo . . . and Speed's didn't need pressing at all. Now why did you want to get rid of me so quickly—and what did you want in that drawer?"

"You'd have to prove I was in that drawer!" challenged Jerry.

"I don't know as I would. All I'd have to do would be to mention it to Speed. He thinks there's something flukey about this, anyway."

"Listen, Ronnie—if you know what's good for you—you'll keep still! I don't have to explain my actions to you. Speed's already upset enough over what's happened—and the big game of the year's only four days off. Now, if you want to see him lose it—just make all the trouble you can!"

"I don't want him to lose but I don't want him to blame me, either. Speed's one of the finest fellows I've ever met. I'd do anything for him."

"All right!" said Jerry, sharply. "Think it over, then. Speed's gotten his stolen property back . . . so have I. So we're not out anything but the experience. If you're set on accusing me you might, out of consideration for Speed, hold off till after the game. Sorry—I've got to be running!"

With that, Jerry was off on a dog trot across the campus, leaving a badly perplexed Ronald Cooper staring fixedly after him.

"Now, what?" asked Jerry Martin, Wednesday night, as his room-mate returned from answering the door. Jerry had been deep in a book and had paid no attention to proceedings but now, on looking up, he perceived that Speed was opening a letter.

"What? Another special?"

Speed, pale of face, nodded. He was studying the contents of the letter intently, lips moving.

"Well!" Jerry exclaimed, throwing down his book. "Here's where I jump out the window! Is it from the same tormentor? Excuse me—I know you say it's none of my business but . . . good grief, man—you're white as a sheet! Here—sit down!"

Jerry shoved a chair forward and Speed reached for it to steady himself. Without a word he passed the letter over. Jerry took it, burning with curiosity, and glanced at the contents.

Dear Mr. Durgan:

You might be interested to know that an attempt is going to be made to kidnap you Friday so you can't pitch for Billiter in the championship game.

A Friend.

"Whoa!" gasped Jerry, doing a stagger act of his own. "Where's a chair for *me*? . . . Good night! What's coming off here? . . . If your other letters have been anything like this . . . I . . . er . . . I wouldn't blame you for being up in the air! Better show this to the Coach right away . . . and call the police. Is the door locked? How about the transom? Oh—I see—it says the kidnapping won't take place till Friday. Well, that gives you a day of freedom yet. Do you suppose this is a Winston trick? Somebody trying to intimidate you? Maybe this guy, Bimbo, who came from your home town . . . ?"

Jerry hazarded much in his erratic comments and questioning but Speed was too disturbed to sense anything.

"No, this isn't from Bimbo," he replied. "I know his handwriting. Besides, he's not afraid of my pitching. That is—I don't think he is!" Speed paused and pursed his lips, thoughtfully. An idea had just occurred to him. Could it be that Bimbo actually did fear him and was conducting this intimidation campaign, as Jerry had suggested, for the purpose of throwing him off form so he could hit him? Speed's heart leaped. There might be something to this! But then again—this letter had been mailed from Crosby, a sizeable city over a hundred miles from Winston. A threat of kidnapping seemed to be going pretty far! Would Bimbo dare do such a thing? Would he be that poor a sport? A personal feud was different—but this anonymous letter suggested possible violence.

"It must be a hoax," calmed Jerry, after the first reaction to the warning was over. "I'd let the Coach know about it but, so far as I was concerned, I'd disregard it."

"Yes, *you would!*" rejoined Speed, feelingly. "It's easy to hand out advice when you're not the one involved. If this letter was addressed to you, I can see you surrounded with bodyguards!"

"Naturally," grinned Jerry. "Because, with the bodyguards, I could *really* disregard the matter!"

"Maybe that's what *I* need!" was Speed's comment.

Coach Thacker, while he appeared to take the threat lightly when consulted by his pitching ace, nevertheless privately commissioned Speed's room-mate not to let Speed out of his sight until game time.

"There's no telling what may be behind this," the coach told Jerry. "Don't let Speed tumble to the fact that you're watching him. I'll try, meanwhile, to have this letter traced down. And I'll also quietly tip off the team to be on the look-out for trouble. Then if there should be a kidnapping attempt, the fellows will be prepared to help Speed out."

Thursday morning a little knot of baseball men gathered on the Billiter campus to secretly discuss the latest sensation—rumor kidnapping of Speed Durgan. They had pledged their coach to keep the rumor strictly among themselves.

"How is Speed taking it?" catcher Ed Keller asked of Jerry.

"Pretty good so far," reported the pitching star's room-mate. "I've had to practically abandon my many activities to trail him, though. I'm glad the game will soon be over. This tracking a fellow all around may be sport for a dog but it's no fun for me. Speed's in the library now and I've got one eye on the main entrance. If any suspicious character saunters up I'm going to hit him first and find out what he's there for afterwards. Of course Friday's supposed to be the day."

"I think it's all a lot of noise!" scoffed short-stop Bert Carver. "This business of kidnapping pitchers may have gone good in the old days. Now, if they want to put 'em out of the way they put poison in their coffee or plant a bomb in their room!"

"Hey! Hey!" protested Jerry. "Lasso that imagination of yours! Speed doesn't care so much for coffee and I often drink his for my second cup. As for bombs—my bed is nearest the door! I prefer that he be kidnapped!"

The fellows laughed.

"Hello!" exclaimed first baseman Dan Lawrence. "There comes that Freshie who looks like Speed's twin brother! Maybe if Speed's really grabbed, we can use *him!*"

"He'd sure look the part," admitted third baseman Pete Osborne. "But they'd rule him off the field when he took his sewing basket to the pitcher's mound!"

"He's not a bad sort," defended Jerry. "And

you guys have just given me a swell idea. Coach pledged us not to tell anyone about this but Ronnie's perfectly safe. What do you say we proposition him to impersonate Speed tomorrow on the chance that he'll be kidnapped instead, if anything like that is really pulled off?"

"Great!" seconded the team members.

"Okay—I'll call Speed's double over."

Ronnie Cooper responded to the summons, pleased at being recognized by five members of Billiter's Varsity nine.

"Hello, fellows!" he greeted, with a nod to Jerry. "What's up?"

"You'd be surprised," said first baseman Lawrence. "Give him the sad news, Jerry."

"Listen, Ronnie, old boy," addressed Jerry. "I don't know what you think of me but I *do* know what you think of Speed . . . and I'm here to tell you that Speed's in a bad spot. This is a dead secret with the team but Coach Thacker's had a tip that there's a plan on foot to kidnap Speed and keep him from pitching against Winston on Saturday."

"N—no!" exclaimed Ronnie, shocked. "You're joking!"

"Do we look it?" barked catcher Ed Keller. "This is darn serious!"

"You bet it is!" seconded Jerry, as Ronnie's eyes widened. "Do you remember, Ronnie, when you were asking me about the Three Arts Club?"

"Why—why, yes, I do!"

"You told me, I believe, that you were very much interested in the stage? And I told you that sometimes a fellow in his first year here gets the opportunity to qualify as a member!"

"That's right!" nodded Ronnie, eagerly. "I remember. But I—I must say I don't see the connection between the—the Three Arts Club and the threat of Speed's being kidnapped?"

"You don't but you will soon!" said Jerry. "I'm about to enlighten you. It just happens that you've the great good fortune to look enough like Billiter's great pitcher to be mistaken for him. That's no longer news—but the fact that you resemble Speed so closely makes you an ideal subject for this . . . er . . . supreme chance to serve your college and its team at a time when a baseball championship hangs in the balance . . . !"

Jerry, taking pains to dramatize the situation, paused a moment to see what affect his words were having. Ronnie's mouth was half open as he stared, trying to comprehend just what was being proposed.

"You—you mean that I—that I'm to let myself be kidnapped in place of—of Speed?" he asked, unbelievingly.

"How did you guess it?" commended Jerry. "Can you imagine that, guys? Ronnie Cooper steps forward and *volunteers* to pose as Speed Durgan . . . to make himself conspicuous on the campus and around the side streets of the college tomorrow . . . so that, if there is a real kidnapping pulled off—he'll be the one they get—and not Billiter's pitching ace! Fellows, I call that one of the finest gestures ever made by a Billiter man! Not only that—if Ronnie should be kidnapped . . . and if he can make his kidnappers believe that he actually is the great Speed Durgan . . . he will prove to the college and especially to the Three Arts Club, that he's an excellent actor. I, myself, under those circumstances, would entertain a petition to get him pledged for the Club and taken in as a full-fledged member at the start of his Sophomore year!"

"You'd do *that* for Ronnie?" took up short-stop Bert Carver. "Say—I wish you'd do the same for me. Here I'm a Junior and I've always wanted to make the Three Arts Club but you've got to get invited to be made a member of it and I've never gotten the chance to show what I could do. Boy, if I'd only had the opportunity that Ronnie has!"

"Ought to be a cinch for him to act like he's Speed, too!" encouraged third baseman Pete Osborne. "He doesn't even have to make up for the part—except to take off those spats. Speed never wore spats!"

Ronnie glanced down at the spats in dismay.

"Well, I—I could take them off. B—but mightn't this kidnapping be dangerous?"

"Naw—you won't be harmed!" assured Jerry. "Of course, mind you, there may not be any kidnapping . . . but we can't afford to have Speed taken if there is. All the kidnappers would want to do would be to keep you captive till after the game. And when you got back to college you'd be a hero! You could easily be the means of Billiter's winning the championship. You might even be awarded a letter!"

"You—you think so?" asked Ronnie, dubiously, glancing from one team member to another.

"You'd be the most talked of man on the campus!" declared catcher Ed Keller. "There's no doubt about it. Have you got the nerve?"

"It doesn't take nerve!" said Jerry, quickly. "All it takes is a fellow who's willing to put in the time. Of course nobody but Ronnie could double for Speed and have a chance of making his captors believe it. But you'd better have some reading matter in your pocket if you decide to go in for this, because you'll have to kill most of the day Saturday wherever they take you."

"Ronnie nodded. "I like to read, too. Who's apt to do this kidnapping—Winston?"

"We don't know," answered Jerry, truthfully. "How about it, Ronnie? Will you do it? Will you sacrifice yourself, if necessary, for Speed?"

The Freshman hesitated, moistening lips that had suddenly become dry. "I—I'll try," he said, finally.

"Good boy—put her there!" cried Jerry, grabbing Ronnie's hand.

Fellow team-mates followed with hearty handshakes and Ronnie's face beamed at the cordiality shown him.

"You're one of the gang from now on!" Jerry assured. "Now, listen—I'll keep Speed off the campus and street as much as I can tomorrow and you dress as near like him as you can. Better yet—I'll sneak some of Speed's clothes over to you. But don't tell a soul about this, understand?"

"I won't," Ronnie promised. "I'll be glad to do this for more than one reason. Maybe, if I am kidnapped, Speed will realize then that I didn't have anything to do with. . . . !"

"Yes, that's right!" cut short Jerry, warningly. "I get you, Ronnie! Now is everything all set? . . . Okay! Then I'll be seeing you tonight!"

"Goodbye, fellows!" said the Freshie who looked like Speed Durgan. "I hope I'm able to help. I hope I make good!"

"The poor sap!" breathed Jerry, watching after Ronnie. "For his sake, I hope this kidnapping doesn't come off!"

"So do I!" laughed catcher Ed Keller. "But, Jerry, you old rascal! You could sell an Eskimo ice!"

CHAPTER XI

A DOUBLE DISAPPEARANCE

NEVER before in the history of the Little Valley Conference had so much interest been manifested in a championship contest. Never before, according to sports writers, had two such outstanding conference nines met for the title. Winston, led by Bimbo Bailey, leading slugger of the Conference and contender for new home run honors, was doped to present the strongest offensive. Billiter was expected to offset this batting advantage by its pitching star, Speed Durgan, who—despite his apparent let-down near the end of the season—was rated as next to invincible at his best. And there were no sports authorities who would predict that Speed would be other than his best for this classic encounter.

"The clash between the Conference's champion batter and champion pitcher should, in itself, be worth traveling miles to see," one sports reporter declared. He might well have been writing with his tongue in his cheek, had he known the possible drama lurking in the rivalry between these two star players.

As the distance between Winston and Billiter was only a matter of some fifty miles, the Billiter squad was to leave by bus at nine Saturday morning with a good percentage of the student body following by special train. Betting favored Winston slightly, probably due to the fact that the game was to be played on Winston's home grounds. Then, too, some of Bimbo Bailey's most prodigious batting feats had been performed there.

"No, siree, Speed—we're sticking in to-night!" said Jerry, commandingly. "It's Friday evening and the goblins are out! We're taking no chances parting company suddenly . . . not with the big game tomorrow. We've got to turn in early, anyway!"

"But I just want to run out for fifteen minutes!" protested Speed.

"Tell me where and I'll do the running for you!" volunteered Jerry.

"Is the world coming to an end?" laughed Speed. "Since when would you do the running for anybody—even yourself?"

"In an emergency!" replied Jerry. "A national emergency—and this is it!"

"Sorry! I've got to do it myself!"

"You're not leaving this room if I have to call the police. I'm not afraid, understand, but I'm just playing safe. That note may have been all the bunk. I thought so from the start and I still think so—but you're the only real pitcher we've got and the fellows made me promise to look after you! So, whether you like it or not, I'm your guardian for this evening! What would you like me to read you: 'Alice in Wonderland'?"

"You get out of my way and cut this nonsense. I'd like to see anybody try to kidnap me. I feel like some excitement tonight. If you want to you can come along but. . . !"

Speed had started for the door. As he did so there were sounds of quick footsteps in the hall, excited voices, then a sharp rapping on the door. The knob turned and catcher Ed Keller looked in.

"Hey, you guys! Heard the news?"

"No! What?" cried Speed and Jerry in one breath.

"Ronnie's been kidnapped!"

"Ronnie?" cried Speed, momentarily bewildered. "But what would they . . . ? Oh, I see! They mistook him for *me!*"

"Great guns!" gasped Jerry. "Then that kidnapping tip was on the level! How'd it happen? Where was he? Anyone see it?"

"I saw it!" declared first baseman Dan Lawrence. "Me and Pete saw it. We were walking down Maple street on the way to the postoffice when we spotted Ronnie sauntering along half a block ahead of us. At least we thought it was Ronnie. He looked so much like Speed we couldn't make sure. And just as he got to the alleyway—that extra dark spot near the vacant lot—a car whizzed out—three men jumped off the running board and threw a blanket over him. He let out one holler but he never had a chance to even put up a struggle. They had him in the back of that car as quick as a wink—so quick that we didn't have a chance to go to his rescue!"

"Did you get the license number of the car?" asked Speed, anxiously.

"No. The rear light was out. It turned away

from us, anyway. It was all over so fast that we thought maybe we'd been seeing things. But we spread the alarm."

"How did you spread it?" demanded Jerry.

"Reported that *Speed* had been kidnapped, of course!" grinned Dan. "Boy, what a thrill this is!"

"Good!" cried Jerry. "You mean—what a martyr Ronnie is!"

"Poor Ronnie!" exclaimed Speed, greatly concerned.

"Poor Ronnie, nothing!" said Jerry. "He got just what he bargained for. That's part of my master-minding. I gave him one of your suits and had him parade around tonight as bait for any kidnappers who might be prowling around! How's that for turning the tables? Now all you've got to do is lay low till game time to-morrow—let the world-at-large think you've actually been kidnapped—and then walk out on the diamond and make Winston fall over dead!"

Speed nodded, grimly. "It's pretty tough on Ronnie," he said, bitterly. "If Winston . . . if Bimbo . . . whoever's behind this is going to pay dearly. I'm going to pitch tomorrow as I've never pitched before!"

"That's the way to talk!" said catcher Ed Keller. "You've got the stuff, Speed. Get mad! The madder, the better!"

"I don't have to get mad!" Speed assured, "I *am* mad!"

"You can't stay here tonight after what's happened," advised Jerry. "There'll be a flock of fellows coming around to inquire as soon as this thing becomes widely known. We few here are the only ones who are in on Ronnie's doubling for you. What we've got to do is get you to Coach Thacker's room as quickly as possible and keep you hidden there! He'll be all for this, I'm certain!"

"But won't something be done to get Ronnie?" persisted Speed. "No telling what those hoodlums will do to him!"

"Don't you worry about Ronnie! He's probably having the time of his life! And they might as well look for him under your name because Ronnie won't admit that he's anyone else. He's going to be Speed Durgan till after game time tomorrow if they half kill him! I talked to him last night and if anyone had resolution in their eyes, he had it. He was ready to die for old Billiter . . . so think of him when you're out there on the mound tomorrow, Speed, and every time that big stiff Bimbo comes to bat, put him down on strikes! I wouldn't be surprised if he was behind all this! He sounds like just the sort of guy who'd pull such stunts! But, come on with me—we've got to slip you out without anyone else seeing you. Run on ahead, Eddie, and see if the coast is clear. Here, Speed, want your night shirt?"

President Eldridge of Winston College was shocked at receipt of a telephone call late Friday night to the effect that Speed Durgan, Billiter's star pitcher, had been abducted from near the rival college campus by some rowdies in a car who were thought to be Winston men.

"I'll investigate this matter at once," the President promised. "But I feel safe in saying now that I am sure no student or students at Winston would stoop to any such practice!"

The investigation, carried into Saturday morning, brought forth an official statement that the Winston faculty was certain none of the student body was implicated in the kidnapping.

"It is our belief that this unfortunate and criminally libelous act was committed by accomplices of a betting ring which has placed large sums of money on Winston to win and wishes to make these winnings certain," the statement went on to declare.

The kidnapping itself received headline notice in newspapers throughout the country with pictures of the missing hurler. To all appearances, Speed Durgan had been swallowed up in the night following his capture. Only two eye witnesses to the actual kidnapping had come forward, Dan Lawrence and Pete Osborne, both—as it happened—fellow members of the team. They had rushed to Speed's rescue but the car had sped away before they could reach it. Police throughout the state and neighboring states were on the look-out for a large, dark-colored sedan. No satisfactory description of the men was available. They were probably four in number, three actual abductors and the man at the wheel.

"With Speed Durgan out of the box, Billiter's chances are nil!" most sports writers conceded.

"Whoever was responsible for the kidnapping evidently realized this fully in attempting to make a Winston victory certain."

Indignation ran high in Billiter with gloom and consternation commingled. The bottom had fallen out of championship hopes in one fell swoop and concern was felt for the safety of Speed Durgan. Billiter rooters, arriving in Winston, were pardoned by sympathetic Winston supporters for voicing suspicion of them.

"We know exactly how Billiter feels about this," one prominent Winstonite expressed. "We probably *would* be feeling the same toward Billiter if, for instance, our hard-hitting Bimbo Bailey had been spirited away."

There was one student in Winston College who suffered a great personal shock at news of Speed Durgan's abduction. Marjory Coulter had looked forward to seeing Speed at the game, secretly interested in noting whether any change had come over him . . . how he would conduct himself in this next clash with Bimbo. And now the much anticipated meeting could not be—a dark shadow had been cast over the entire game. Marjory was sure there was not a true sportsman who would experience real joy in defeating Billiter with Speed Durgan out of the line-up. On taking her seat at the game, she watched her chance and motioned Bimbo over to her as he was standing in line for batting practice.

"Has there been any word about Speed?" she asked, guardedly.

"I haven't heard anything," said Bimbo, frankly. "Tried to find out, too. I asked some of the Billiter fellows in the clubhouse. It's an outrage, isn't it? I'd give anything if this hadn't happened! I'll bet Speed's thinking, wherever he is, that I'm in some way responsible."

"Why should he?"

"Well . . . I . . . er . . . . I've probably given him good reason for thinking so one time and another," confessed Bimbo, shamefacedly. "I got a kick out of razzing him but now that this has broken . . . !"

"Look at me, Bimbo!" commanded Marjory. "Are you sure that no Winston fellows are behind Speed's disappearance?"

"If they are," answered Bimbo, unflinchingly, "I don't know anything about it!"

"Who's going to pitch for Billiter?"

"A guy by the name of Ray Chapman. He's warming up over there now. See him?"

Marjory looked across the diamond at a long, lanky youth who was winding up slowly and pitching lazily to catcher Ed Keller.

"He doesn't look like so much," she observed.

"He's a slow ball artist," grinned Bimbo. "He won't last long with us!"

"This game ought to be called off!" declared Marjory, feelingly. "It doesn't seem fair to be playing this way!"

"Well, it's my turn at batting practice," said Bimbo, excusing himself. "Don't forget— you're going to the party with me tonight. It's being given in honor of the Billiter team and maybe Speed will have shown up by that time. If he has, I'll try to make up to him by giving him a dance with you!"

Marjory waved Bimbo away, feigning provocation.

"Batteries for today's game!" announced the umpire as a breathless stillness fell over the packed stands. "For Winston: Ferris and O'Reilly; for Billiter, Chapman and Keller. Play ball!"

Billiter, as the visiting team, was first at bat. The air hung heavy with excitement. Anything might happen in the dramatic setting that had been provided for this championship conflict. The Billiter team members had been showing a pep and fight in practice which indicated that they were going to battle heroically to make up for the loss of their pitching star. And a cheer went up as Jerry Martin, Billiter's lead-off hitter, strode to the plate. But, though the first three Billiter batters hit the ball hard, it was driven directly into the hands of Winston fielders and Jack Ferris, Winston pitcher, retired the side in order.

"Good start for us!" opined a Winston fan. "Now let's see what Billiter's relief pitcher can do to our batters!"

But, before Ray Chapman could take the mound, wild cries directed the crowd's attention to the field house out near the fence, from which a uniformed figure was seen to come running.

"It's Speed Durgan!" yelled the Billiter stands. "What do you know about that? Yea, Speed!"

A hundred and one varieties of pandemonium

broke loose with the Winston crowd providing as noisy a greeting as Speed's own supporters. Billiter's pitching ace acknowledged the terrific ovation with a lifting of the hand and was enveloped in a joyous mass of his own team-mates who made his reception look very spontaneous and real.

"I'm all warmed up," Speed told his fellows, winking at a wise Coach Thacker. "Who do you think caught me? Detective Hall! In a cow pasture just outside of town. Then he brought me here in his car just in time to catch the game and reporters are out there in the clubhouse trying to get the story from him as to how he rescued me from kidnappers!"

"Better take another short warm-up," advised the Coach. "I'll arrange with Winston."

"Oh, Speed! Yoo hoo!" cried a girlish voice, as Billiter's pitching star stalked to the mound with the stands an excited murmur of sound.

Speed turned his head in the direction of the voice and caught sight of Marjory. His face lighted and he nodded his recognition. Bimbo Bailey came rushing from the Winston dugout and across the diamond, extending his hand in a gesture of welcome.

"Mighty glad to see you Speed!" he said, on approaching him. "Awfully sorry this happened!"

"Yes you are!" snapped an aroused Speed Durgan, and the crowd gasped as he strode past the mighty Bimbo, refusing to shake hands!

For once in his life Bimbo seemed actually stunned by the incident, occurring as it had in full view of the hundreds in the stands—an open indication of the feud between the two— and also suggesting that Speed was holding him accountable for a part in the kidnapping. Bimbo took an angry step after Billiter's pitching ace, then evidently thought better of prolonging the scene, wheeling about instead and kicking up dust with his cleats as he returned to the Winston dugout and picked up his bat.

"There's fur going to fly now!" someone predicted.

"But Speed Durgan, burning with the desire to avenge the kidnapping of the fellow who had looked like him, was in his rarest form. Ronnie Cooper had believed in him; had seen himself in the shoes of his idol. Wherever Ronnie was now, he was probably playing Speed's part, making his captors think he was frantic to get his release and take part in the game, when Ronnie could perhaps not so much as throw a ball over the plate.

"I'll make 'em sorry they ever pulled this stunt!" Speed vowed, and forthwith proceeded to strike out the head of Winston's batting order—all three batters going down, swinging.

"Is he *hot?*" shrilled a rabid Billiter fan. "Say—he's liable to break all world's records and strike out twenty-seven men in a row!"

This remark brought a big laugh and Speed Durgan received tumultuous applause as he left the mound. Wondering glances followed him, however, as he stopped in front of the Winston bleachers and engaged in conversation with a girl wearing Winston colors who greeted him cordially.

"Listen, Marj!" Speed said, in a low voice. "Winston's throwing a party for us tonight, as you know. How about your going with me?"

"But I—I've promised Bimbo!" said Marjory, reluctantly.

"Turn about's fair play," pressed Speed. "Bimbo made a bet with you once. Now I'm betting that I beat Bimbo for the privilege of taking you to the party!"

Marjory's eyes danced. "I'll take that bet," she accepted. "I'll tell Bimbo about it when he comes in from the field, if I can call him over. I'm sure he'll be sport enough to agree to it!"

"Good!" said Speed, grimly, and departed before Marjory could ask a question about his kidnapping.

Billiter was unable to do much with the offerings of Jack Ferris, Winston mound artist, and went into the last half of the second inning with Bimbo Bailey, first at bat for the home hopes.

"Oh, Bimbo!" called a voice, as Winston's heavy hitter stepped from the dugout, bat in hand.

Speed Durgan was taking the customary three warm-up pitches. Seeing that he had a moment before going to the plate, Bimbo answered the summons of the co-ed who had been receiving attention from the stars of both nines.

"They're all three from the same town!" informed a wiseacre. "That explains it!"

As Bimbo left Marjory Coulter he was scowling deeply. Already miffed at Speed's shunning of him in public, he was made furious at Speed's audacity in betting on himself to win. This certainly wasn't the Speed of old. Well, he'd show him that he couldn't pull that kind of stuff on Bimbo!

"They're all alike to you today, big boy!" talked catcher Ed Keller to Speed as Winston's batting siege gun took his position at the plate and swung his black club ominously. "This baby's going down on strikes, too!"

CHAPTER XII

A TEST OF NERVE

CRACK!

Reaching out savagely for Speed Durgan's first pitch which had been intended as a teaser, just over the outside corner of the plate, Bimbo Bailey connected with the whizzing horsehide —catching it on the end of his black bat and reversing its direction so swiftly that the ball, when next seen, was traveling on a rising line toward the centerfield fence.

"It's a home run!" shrieked the Winston crowd, whose eyes were practiced on the distances of the home playing field. "There she goes—out of the park! What a smash! The longest hit Bimbo's ever made here!"

Clearing the fence by at least twenty feet, the ball landed in the middle of the street without and bounded upon the porch of a house on the other side, waking a dear old lady from her nap and causing her to scold some entirely innocent but scared young boys who had been playing in the adjacent yard. But the ball accomplished

more than this. In making its spectacular exit
from the ball game, it had—due to the propell-
ing force of one Bimbo Bailey—automatically
broken the long standing home run record of
the Little Valley Conference which had remained a total of 13 since the year nineteen
hundred and seven. This ball was the symbol
of home run number fourteen and it was no
wonder that the small boys, who rescued it at the
peril of further censure from the dear old lady,
were admitted to the game free on presenting
it at the gate for admission.

As for a widely grinning Bimbo, he couldn't
resist an exultant taunt at a greatly dejected
rival on the pitching mound, who watched him
circle the bases.

"Don't you wish you'd stayed kidnapped!"
he called to Speed, as he rounded second.
"Didn't I tell you I'd break the Conference record against you? I'll be seeing you at the party
tonight! Ha! Ha! Ha!"

Speed made no retort to this razzing and
waited quietly on the mound while much ceremony was made over Bimbo's touching of the
home plate—newspaper photographers snap-

ping him as he stepped on it to complete the home run which made history.

"Greatest batter this conference has ever seen!" declared an admirer. "And he pickled Speed's first ball after Speed had struck out our first three batters. What a man! I guess that hasn't ruined Speed's morale for the afternoon!"

The rooter was partially right. Bimbo's tremendous drive had brought the old fear complex back upon Speed. And his next time at bat, the crowd booed as Bimbo was given his base on balls. This was an old expedient which Speed recalled as having proven successful in his last high school game—up to the moment when he had been forced to pitch to Bimbo. And Speed ardently hoped that such a moment would not arrive in this encounter for he was finding it fairly easy to baffle the other Winston batters.

Winston held her one run lead until the fifth when Billiter tied the count on two singles and a sacrifice fly. It was still anybody's game, with Bimbo twice given free tickets to first where he growled and ranted to no good purpose. It was a case of wisdom being the better part of

valor and Speed found himself quite imperv-
ious to the shouts of those who branded him as
"Yellow! . . . Afraid to pitch to him! . . .
Do you call that sportsmanship?" Let the fans
rave. He was pitching this ball game and he intended to win it or die trying . . . win it in
spite of the fact that Speed had his goat!

As Billiter came in from the field to start
the first of the sixth, an attendant from the field
house addressed the players.

"Is one of you fellows named Jerry Martin?"

"That's me!" identified Jerry.

"There's a long distance telephone call for
you, sir! Some young man demanding to talk
to you. He seems very excited. Says his name's
Cooper!"

"Great cats!" exclaimed Jerry. "Let's see
—I just batted last this inning. How about it,
Coach—will I have time to beat it to the field
house and . . . ?"

"Go to it!" said Coach Thacker.

Jerry raced across the field with the attendant at his heels, and Speed yelling something
after which sounded like, "Give my regards to
Ronnie!"

"Hello! Hello!" he gasped into the phone, almost before he had put the dangling receiver to his ear.

"Hello, is this Jerry?"

"Yes, yes—but I'm out of breath. Shoot, Ronnie! There's a ball game going on! Where are you?"

"I—I'm in a telephone booth!"

"I know—but where?"

"In a—in a drug store. I'm in my b. v. d.'s, too!"

"*What?*"

"They took all my clothes from me and when they found I wasn't really the pitcher—they pitched me out on my head!"

"The dirty bums! Who are they—Winston men?"

"No—gamblers!"

"Then they're worse than dirty! What do you want me to do?"

"Get me some clothes and some money! I borrowed money from the druggist here to make this call!"

"What place you calling from?"

"Newcastle!"

Where in blazes is that?"

"Fifteen miles from you!"

"Well, I can't take time to get clothes and money for you. That's a job for the Salvation Army. I mean—I've got to get back to the ball game. You were able to borrow some money— borrow clothes from the druggist, too."

"I—I can't! He's a *woman!*"

Jerry reeled against the wall. "Well, borrow a dress then! Disguise yourself! Do anything to get on here to Winston!"

"A man's just come in the store now. I'll ask him if he has an extra pair of pants."

"Good! Hire someone to bring you on here. We'll stand all expenses. Great stuff, old boy!"

"Wait a minute! Do I get in the Three Arts Club?"

"Yes, sir—on one of the committees! I've got to go now—they tell me the inning's over!"

"*Wait!* How's the game going?"

"Score's a tie, one to one, end of the fifth!"

"Oh, it must be thrilling. I—I'll call you back if I can't get the pants! This is very embarrassing . . ."

"Goodbye and look luck!" shouted Jerry into

the mouth piece, hanging up the receiver and making a dash for the door. "If that bird calls back, tell him I'm out to lunch!"

Team members crowded about Jerry to get the story as he returned to his second base position. Speed was most anxious of all to know what had happened to his "double."

"Ronnie's okay except he's suffering from slight exposure at present with nothing much more than a telephone booth wrapped around him. The kidnappers pushed him out of their car minus everything but his b. v. d.'s. From what he says the men are gamblers who've placed heavy bets on Winston to win. I told Ronnie to beat it on here. He's only fifteen miles away!"

Employing the same safe tactics, Billiter's pitching ace, who had allowed but three scratch hits in addition to Bimbo's home run smash, issued another base on balls to Winston's mighty slugger in the last of the seventh. A great howl of protest went up from disappointed Winston rooters but to no avail. And, when Billiter broke the tie in the first of ninth on a two bagger by Jerry and a single by first baseman Dan Lawrence—the Billiter crowd went wild.

"All we've got to do now is retire three more men and we've got the championship!" yelled a delirious rooter. "Last of the ninth coming up! All right, Speed—you're covering yourself with glory today, old man! Blaze 'em in there! Don't let 'em see that pill this time!"

Speed did not need to be so admonished. This was his very intention—to bear down with all the strength and craftsmanship that he possessed. He was going to break the jinx this time. There was going to be no last minute blow-up. But, as Speed left the dugout to take the mound, an usher stepped up and presented him with a note.

"What's this?" Speed asked, a bit disturbed by the detraction of his attention from the game.

"Gentleman gave it to me for you," apologized the usher. "Said it was very important!"

Speed nodded and opened the note on his way to pitcher's box. He stopped dead still, however, before he had taken half a dozen more steps and stared unbelievingly at what had been scribbled on a yellow sheet of paper.

If you pass Bimbo again—you won't leave this park alive!

The threat sent an unpleasant tingling up and down his spinal cord. His first impulse was to report the matter to the umpire and have him turn the slip of paper over to police. But calmer judgment told him that this would only cause a furor, might even hold up the game, and could make of him a laughing stock. This note had either been inspired by a hard-losing Winstonite or was the product of some fanatic.

"Bimbo's the fourth man to bat this inning," Speed figured. "I may not have to pitch to him at all. If I get the first three batters the game will be over . . ."

But Speed's hope was shattered at once when the first batter singled sharply to right.

"Yea! The tieing run's on base!" shouted Winston. "And Bimbo gets a bat this inning! Goodbye, ball game!"

"Speed's slipping!" cried another.

"Not so you could notice it!" retorted a Billiter rooter, joyously, as the next two Winston batters, trying desperately to bring their comrade on the bases home, succeeded only in getting him around to third on their respective outs at first.

But now a fiendish Bimbo was at the plate
—and all Winston rose up with a frenzied plea
for him to hit the ball out of the lot once more
and win the game!

Speed surveyed the situation, nervously. The
crumpled sheet of yellow paper was in his hip
pocket. The words upon it passed in review before his tortured consciousness: "If you pass
Bimbo again—you won't leave this park alive!"
Was this just an empty threat or might someone
be crazy enough to take a shot at him? There
was catcher Ed Keller, giving him the signal
to walk Bimbo as usual. But Speed, biting his
lips, shook his head. Catcher Keller insisted.
Again Speed shook his head. This brought the
infield about him in protest.

"What's biting you, Speed?" demanded
Jerry. "You lost your head? This is the place
to walk Bimbo of all times. A little single now
ties the score. A homer ends it all. We'll get the
next batter for you. See—there's Coach Thacker
wig-wagging from the bench!"

"I—I've got to pitch to him!" Speed rejoined, a tremor seizing him.

"But you're foolish to take such a risk!"

warned shortstop Bert Carver. "You've struck this next batter out twice. He hasn't made a hit today. He's your meat. But, Bimbo . . . !"

"I've got to pitch to him!" Speed repeated, between clenched teeth.

As he turned toward the batter, grim determination on his face, the stands sensed that he intended to pitch to the mighty Bimbo—to match his pitching skill against Bimbo's great batting ability—and the Winston crowd burst into applause. They'd misjudged the opposing pitcher after all. Any fellow, with the game apparently in the palm of his hand, who would decide to risk it by giving his opponents a fighting chance—deserved plenty of credit. He was a sportsman in a thousand. Speed's face burned as he realized he was getting credit for a courage that he did not merit. He had the uncanny feeling that, somewhere in the crowd, was the crank who had written the threatening note, with fingers, possibly even now, twitching against the trigger of a gun . . . ready to carry out his threat if he should send Bimbo to first on balls. Just as unbelievable things *had* happened. The kidnapping of Ronnie hadn't been any joke!

White of face, Speed released the first ball. He groaned as he saw it go wide of the plate and heard the umpire announce: "Ball one!"

The Winston stands instantly commenced to boo him—all but one—a girl who sat nervously clasping and unclasping her hands . . . watching the figure on the mound and sensing, probably more than anyone else on the field, the struggle that figure was undergoing.

As he raised his arm for the next pitch, there was a sudden, sharp report. Speed dropped his arm, startled, and stepped from the box.

"What was that?" he asked, impulsively. "A shot?"

"Naw!" scoffed first baseman Dan Lawrence. "Just a goofy guy over here in a box who exploded a paper sack!"

Speed stared and nodded, moistening dry lips as he stepped back on the pitcher's slab.

Unnerved, though he had intended to pitch a strike ball, his second pitch also went wide of the plate.

"Atta boy!" called catcher Ed Keller, relieved. "Give him two more like that and ship the big ham down to first!"

But Speed's attention was now centered more on the man in the box than on the batter. As he raised his arms for the next pitch he saw the man Dan had pointed out take another paper sack from his pocket, blow it up and get ready to pop it. Immediately, Speed stepped from the box and appealed to the umpire to call the game.

"What for?" demanded the arbiter.

"There's a man in that box I think's connected with the kidnapping!" said Speed. "I want him arrested on suspicion! He's trying to intimidate me . . . !"

The umpire raised his hand as members of both teams looked on, dumbfoundedly.

"What's up?"

"What's coming off out there?"

But before these questions could be answered, Speed, to the amazement of the crowd, started toward the box in which his annoyer was sitting. At sight of his approach, however, the man leaped from the box, overturning his chair, and cut across the field, racing toward an exit. Unable to catch up to him and with the park in an uproar. Speed took aim and let loose the baseball.

"Look at that! He clipped that guy right in the back of the head—and knocked him out!" cried a spectator.

Second baseman Jerry Martin, though he didn't know what the commotion was all about, had given chase to the fleeing stranger and, upon his being dropped by Speed's accurate aim, Jerry fell on him and held him down. Winston police arrived a moment later and to them Speed gasped out an explanation of his act. The man, coming to, indignantly protested his innocence.

"Then what did you try to beat it for?" demanded a copper.

"That's the man!" cried a voice. "One of them, anyway! Good shot, Speed, old boy!"

Looking about, Speed beheld the figure of Ronnie running up. The Freshie was oddly attired in borrowed clothes several sizes too big. He had just reached the park in time to see the spectacular incident.

"What are you guys—twins?" the man demanded, sullenly, looking bewilderedly from one to the other.

"Come on with us!" ordered the policeman, jerking him toward the sidelines.

"Good boy, Ronnie!" said Speed, turning to his double and patting his hero worshipper on the back. "You're a wonder! You've done your part—now I've got to do mine!"

"Strike him out!" begged Ronnie. "You can do it!"

Speed stared. He had just decided to walk Bimbo, now that his fear of consequences had been removed. There were already two balls on the batter. To win the game was more important than . . .! But, was it? Hadn't he waited all this time . . . and pitched the best he knew how—in the hopes of getting another chance to . . . ? Speed returned to the box, shaken, but with a peculiar determination he had never before experienced. The crowd gave him a great cheer. It resented the attempt to throw him off his game. But the crowd knew nothing of this other form of intimidation which had been going on for years . . . and which was personified by the murderous-looking figure at the plate!

"This is my chance to get past it for all time!" Speed told himself. "If I pass it up again I'll never be able to forgive myself!"

"Walk this baby!" urged catcher Keller.

"You're in no shape to pitch to him, Speed! We'll get the next one for you!"

This assurance had been given Speed before but it still had no effect.

"No, I'm pitching to him!" Speed announced. "This guy's had my goat long enough. I can't stand it any longer!"

His next pitch was one of blinding speed—the kind of ball that had won him his nickname. Bimbo swung his ponderous black bat—and missed.

Two balls and one strike!

"Strike him out!" yelled a crazily attired fellow from the Billiter stands and the Winston crowd laughed.

"He'll never strike the Bimbo out!" said a rooter, confidently. "Nobody's struck him out all season!"

But the next pitch was just as blistering and Bimbo cut the air cleanly on a terrific swing.

Bimbo, surprised at Speed's change of front, stepped from the box and tapped the dirt from his cleats.

"You mean business this time, don't you!" he said, resuming his stance. "Well, so do I!"

"Ball three!" announced the umpire, as the man on third ran down the base line, threatening to go home.

"Bring me in, Bimbo old boy!" he pleaded.

"He's going to lose him!" predicted the crowd. "He's lost his nerve! He's going to give Bimbo a pass!"

Bimbo grinned and nodded his head, contemptuously. "I thought so!" he sneered. "Making a big show! You're afraid to stick another in there!"

But the next pitch was a whiz ball, waist high, which Bimbo swung at and knocked out of the park on a high foul.

"Good night!" cried a spectator. "Better walk him, Speed, before it's too late!"

Agony was prolonged as Bimbo fouled another pitch off.

"Staying with me, are you?" he taunted. "Well, I'll give you credit! But you don't really think you can strike me out, do you? . . . Come on, now—let's see that home run ball!"

With every pitch a greater and greater strain, Speed gathered himself for what he felt must be his last pitch. Above the excited din of the crowd he heard the shrill petition of a girl: "Come on, Speed Durgan! You're going to do it this time! You're going to do it!" . . .

"Strike him out!" came Billiter's frenzied plea, now that the stands thoroughly understood Speed's determination to duel it out to the finish. "Strike him out!"

"Home run, Bimbo! Home run!" appealed all Winston, with a great stamping of feet. "Break up the old ball game! Home run!"

Unbearable suspense as Speed released the ball . . . hearts palpitating in throats as the horsehide approached the plate in a flash of white . . . then a mighty roar as Bimbo swung and turned completely around—while the ball disappeared, not over the fence but—with a resounding smack—in catcher Keller's big mitt.

For a moment all sound died down to a whisper and then a high-pitched voice suddenly shrieked: "He did it! He did it! He struck him out! Yea, Speed!" And Ronnie Cooper stumbled onto the field, holding up a pair of trousers that were several inches too long as he raced toward the fellow he had impersonated, to offer congratulations. In another instant the diamond was swarming with joy-crazed Billiter fans . . .

Speed, who had sunk to one knee from the relief of tension, was quick to recover as Bimbo, proving himself a good and generous sportsman, rushed out to shake his hand. This time Speed took it, warmly.

"Pretty mean of me to ride you the way I did!" Bimbo apologized.

"That's all right," accepted Speed. "I guess I just had to get so fed up on it before I could force myself to do anything about it!"

"I was afraid I might over-play my hand some day," Bimbo grinned. "Say—-how about a dance with Marjory tonight . . . ?"

"Don't give him any!" said Jerry, who had been listening in. "Make him *like* it!"

"I haven't the heart," responded Speed. "Not after Bimbo's *giving* us the championship!"

"Picture me doing that!" rejoined the home run king of the Little Valley Conference. "But you can't blame me for the kidnapping. You know darned well, there's no other pitcher I'd rather face than you . . . that is . . . I mean —*say*, where *is* this bunch of kidnappers? Maybe I can make some arrangement with 'em for *next year* . . . !"